陳幸美◎著

圖解 一次學好
餐飲英語

會話＋句型 附MP3

圖解搭配對話短句：
圖解對話有效輔助學習，短對話省時＋萬用，
適用各種程度的學習者，
用貼近生活的情境學習，效果顯著！

圖解易上手：
十輔助，輕鬆記憶
飲字彙和短句

★省時＋萬用：每個短句均附「拓展句」，
少量時間學會每則句型，輕鬆搞定各種服
務情境。跨餐飲主題一樣好用！

★餐飲一問三答：
組織出更多樣的回答！
從容應對不打結。

Author's Preface
・作 者 序・

　　翻開這本餐飲英語書大家應該會注意到字彙和句子的結構都非常淺顯易懂，這也是寫這本書的本意，希望大家能夠用簡單的字彙精準的表達到位！自助旅行的風氣盛行之下，大家也願意自己訂飯店，自己找景點，這比起團體旅遊更多了一份冒險的感覺，但卻又可能會不如預期的出錯。這本餐飲英語書可以幫您解決許多出門在外遇到的問題，教您如何用簡單的字彙向相關人員反應問題。

　　寫這本書的角度，除了是站喜歡自助旅行的夥伴們立場，希望能夠更容易表達自己心裡的想法，找到想住的房型，吃到喜歡的料理，減少雞同鴨講的窘境；更是站在餐飲同業人員的角度，如何能輕易地跟外國人解釋博大精深的中式料理，對於在餐飲或是飯店業服務工作人員在面對外國客人上絕對非常有幫助！

陳幸美 敬上

在工作、生活或旅遊中餐飲英語的範圍極廣,其實很多時候不見得要學非常多的表達句型和語彙就能達到溝通的效果。觀看網路 po 文等,常會看到有些旅遊者表達出講錯點飲料時,「少冰」、「少糖」等等的用語,然後 po 文的圖片旁就出現了,「你看,然後飲料就變只剩這樣」。Po 文除了讓人感到新奇好玩和吸引朋友回覆之外,其實也會思考著自己學了那麼多年英語,但對於面對許多生活層面的「實用」、「解決問題」的英語表達內容卻啞口無言。

雖然有時候會有人好心提供解答,但其實非常片段,而編輯部這次彙整了許多可能學習者感到興趣且即好上手的英語短句提供許多學習者參考,在短時間內就能達到學習成效,即刻於旅遊時使用。最後要感謝作者陳幸美自**雅思口說**和**國貿英語書**後又寫了這本英語道地又實用的書籍。

倍斯特編輯部 敬上

UNIT **1**

冰塊

★ **情境簡述**

在點冷飲的時候會遇到最大的問題就是要多冰呢? 在台灣對冰塊的選擇性還真不少,例如多冰 (Extra ice)、正常冰 (Standard ice)、少冰 (Less ice)、去冰 (No ice)。常常拿到飲料的時候才發現冰塊比飲料多,真是欲哭無淚啊! 這個單元就來解決這個問題吧!

UNIT 1　冰塊

Part 01 圖解實用短句50篇

★ **情境對話** MP3-001

Rita: Can I have a plum green tea please?
Cameron: Large, regular or small?
Rita: How big is large?
Cameron: It is 750cc for the large. 500cc for the regular and 350cc for the small.
Rita: Oh, just a regular one then please.
Cameron: One regular plum green tea with standard ice?
Rita: I will have less ice instead. Thanks.

瑞　塔: 您好,一杯梅子綠茶。
卡麥倫: 要大杯中杯還是小杯?
瑞　塔: 請問大杯是多大杯?
卡麥倫: 大杯是 750cc,中杯是 500cc,小杯是 350cc。
瑞　塔: 那中杯的就好,謝謝。
卡麥倫: 一杯中杯梅子綠茶正常冰嗎?
瑞　塔: 麻煩你少冰。

015

- 迅速了解每個單元的內容,學習與單元主題相關的超實用字彙和片語。

- 學習道地對話,旅遊、點餐、餐飲工作均適用,面對各種狀況均不鬧笑話。

- 圖解式呈現，搭配圖片更易學，每個圖片均搭配各主題字彙與例句，充分運用該主題字彙到句型使用中。

- 此外，每個主題更附兩句「還能怎麼說」，強化句型「換句話說」、「同義表達」的能力，增添口說風采，快點來偷學幾句吧！

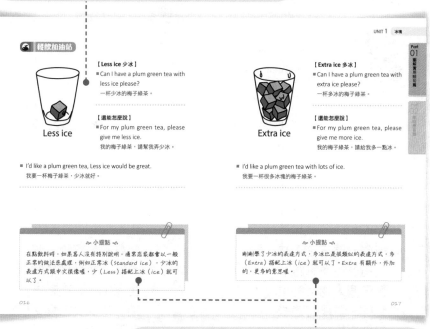

🍴 餐飲加油站

【Less ice 少冰】
- Can I have a plum green tea with less ice please?
  一杯少冰的梅子綠茶。

【還能怎麼說】
- For my plum green tea, please give me less ice.
  我的梅子綠茶，請幫我弄少冰。

Less ice

- I'd like a plum green tea, Less ice would be great.
  我要一杯梅子綠茶，少冰就好。

【Extra ice 多冰】
- Can I have a plum green tea with extra ice please?
  一杯多冰的梅子綠茶。

【還能怎麼說】
- For my plum green tea, please give me more ice.
  我的梅子綠茶，請給我多一點冰。

Extra ice

- I'd like a plum green tea with lots of ice.
  我要一杯很多冰塊的梅子綠茶。

📎 小提點 📎

在點飲料時，如果客人沒有特別說明，通常店家都會以一般正常的做法來處理，例如正常冰（Standard ice），少冰的表達方式就跟中文很像喔，少（Less）搭配上冰（ice）就可以了。

📎 小提點 📎

剛剛學了少冰的表達方式，多冰也是很類似的表達方式，多（Extra）搭配上冰（ice）就可以了。Extra 有額外，外加的，更多的意思喔。

- 小提點收錄更多需要注意的地方，學會更多延伸相關用語，例如：咖啡濃度的講法，進一步拓展到1/2、1/4濃度的講法為何，快速飆升餐飲口說能力。

UNIT 1 飯店訂位和座位

一問三答 MP3 026

Q1 Can we have the lounge area?
可以坐沙發區嗎？

Audrey Well, our lounge area is quite small, it is designed for maximum 4 people, and there are 6 of you, I would suggest the round table, there is more room for everyone.

奧黛莉　嗯，我們的沙發區很小，大概只能坐 4 個人，而你們有六個，我會建議你們坐圓桌，這樣位子比較大。

Sabrina Of course you can. But I need to remind you the table in the lounge area is very low, it is difficult to have meals there.

莎賓娜　當然可以，只是我要提醒您，我們沙發區的桌子很低，如果要吃餐點會不方便。

Dexter Sorry the lounge area is booked out, but we got a nice outdoor area with big chairs, it is quite nice, too. Do you want me to reserve for you?

戴斯特　抱歉沙發區已經有預訂了，我們的戶外區也很不錯，椅子大又舒服。要不要預約戶外區？

字彙表

round table	圓桌
lounge area	沙發區
outdoor area	戶外區
booked out	訂滿了

MEMO

118

119

Part 02 即時應生篇

- 規劃一問三答，有效拓展答題思路，從三個人物回答中偷師，並能將這些句型組織並運用在其他相關回答中。（反覆聽音檔效果更佳。）

- 精選餐飲字彙，背包客、餐飲科系學生最佳的字彙指南，背少少字彙就能趴趴走！

・UNIT 1・
飯店訂位和座位

超實用短句 1

❶ 我想要訂位
⇨ would like to make a reservation.

❷ 你們星期五晚上還有空位嗎?
⇨ Are you fully booked this Friday night?

❸ 可以幫我留一張兩個人的桌子嗎?
⇨ Can I have a table for two please?

❹ 我想要靠窗的桌子。
⇨ I would prefer the table by the window.

超實用短句 2

❶ 我們一共六個人
⇨ We are a party of 6.

❷ 需不需要先付訂金?
⇨ Do you require any deposit?

❸ 我們需要兩個兒童餐椅
⇨ We need two high chairs.

❹ 我不要靠近廁所的位置
⇨ I prefer somewhere away from the toilet.

Part 02 即時應答篇

MEMO

- 最易上手的餐飲短句,能即刻用於餐飲職場情境中。
- 最省時的學習,基礎款句型學會就能嚇嚇叫!

·目次·CONTENTS

 PART 1　圖解實用短句篇

CONTENTS

PART 2　即時應答篇

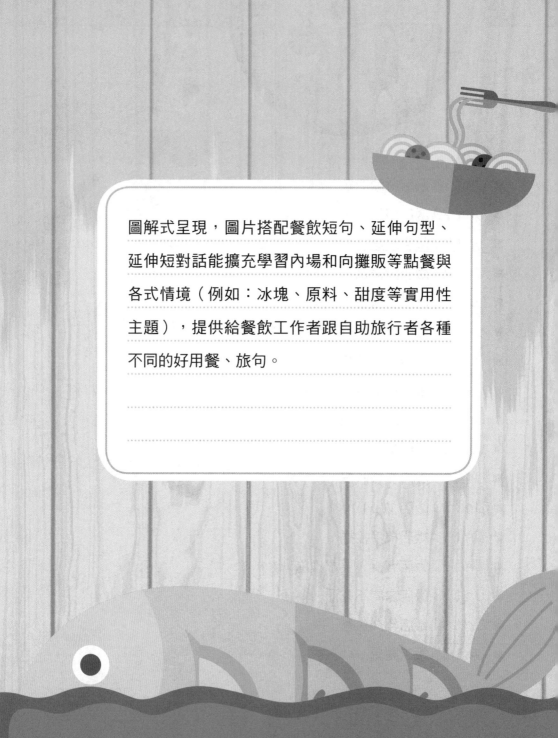

圖解式呈現，圖片搭配餐飲短句、延伸句型、延伸短對話能擴充學習內場和向攤販等點餐與各式情境（例如：冰塊、原料、甜度等實用性主題），提供給餐飲工作者跟自助旅行者各種不同的好用餐、旅句。

PART 1

· 圖解實用短句篇 ·

冰塊

★ 情境概述

在點冷飲的時候會遇到最大的問題就是要多冰呢？在台灣對冰塊的選擇性還真不少，例如多冰（Extra ice）、正常冰（Standard ice）、少冰（Less ice）、去冰（No ice）。常常拿到飲料的時候才發現冰塊比飲料多，真是欲哭無淚啊！這個單元就來解決這個問題吧！

🍴 情境對話　MP3 001

Rita:　　　Can I have a plum green tea please?

Cameron: Large, regular or small?

Rita:　　　How big is large?

Cameron: It is 750cc for the large. 500cc for the regular and 350cc for the small.

Rita:　　　Oh, just a regular one then please.

Cameron: One regular plum green tea with standard ice?

Rita:　　　I will have less ice instead. Thanks.

Part **01** 圖解實用短句篇

Part **02** 即時應答篇

瑞　塔：您好，一杯梅子綠茶。

卡麥倫：要大杯中杯還是小杯？

瑞　塔：請問大杯是多大杯？

卡麥倫：大杯是 750cc、中杯是 500cc、小杯是 350cc。

瑞　塔：那中杯的就好，謝謝。

卡麥倫：一杯中杯梅子綠茶正常冰嗎？

瑞　塔：麻煩你少冰。

Less ice

【Less ice 少冰】

■ Can I have a plum green tea with less ice please?

一杯少冰的梅子綠茶。

【還能怎麼說】

■ For my plum green tea, please give me less ice.

我的梅子綠茶，請幫我弄少冰。

■ I'd like a plum green tea. Less ice would be great.

我要一杯梅子綠茶，少冰就好。

❧ 小提點 ❧

在點飲料時，如果客人沒有特別說明，通常店家都會以一般正常的作法來處理，例如正常冰（Standard ice），少冰的表達方式跟中文很像喔，少（Less）搭配上冰（ice）就可以了。

Extra ice

【 Extra ice 多冰 】

■ Can I have a plum green tea with extra ice please?
一杯多冰的梅子綠茶。

【 還能怎麼說 】

■ For my plum green tea, please give me more ice.
我的梅子綠茶，請給我多一點冰。

■ I'd like a plum green tea with lots of ice.
我要一杯很多冰塊的梅子綠茶。

⁓ 小提點 ⁓

剛剛學了少冰的表達方式，多冰也是很類似的表達方式，多（Extra）搭配上冰（ice）就可以了。Extra 有額外、外加的、更多的意思喔。

UNIT 2

麵的種類

★ 情境概述

　　在我們的一天三餐中，麵食是一個受歡迎的品項！從來沒想過麵的種類有那麼多。以粗細來説，可以分為寬麵（Fettucini）、中寬麵（Linguine）及細麵（Spaghetti / Thin noodle）。以原料來分還有油麵（Hokkien noodle）、蛋麵（Egg noodle）、米粉（Bihon/ rice noodle）、粿條（Kway Teow / flat rice noodle）、冬粉（Vermicelli / glass noodle）。不過是想點碗麵而已嘛，有這麼困難嗎？

🍴 **情境對話** MP3 002

Sarah: Wow, there are so many to choose from, what is that called?

Ryan: That is dry noodle with pork gravy. You can also have it as a soup noodle if you want. We also make it with rice noodle or vermicelli.

Sarah: That looks good, I think I will try that. I will have what he is having, thanks.

莎拉：哇，有這麼多選擇啊!請問那個是什麼？

萊恩：那是乾的陽春麵，你要做湯的也可以。也可以搭配米粉或是冬粉。

莎拉：那個看起來很好吃，我想試試看，我要一份跟他一樣的，謝謝。

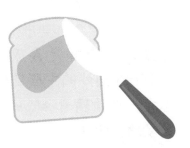

Noodle soup

【noodle soup 湯麵】

■ Can I have a noodle soup with chicken please?

請給我一碗雞肉湯麵，謝謝。

【還能怎麼說】

■ One noodle soup and please add chicken.

一碗湯麵，請加雞肉。

■ I would like to order a chicken soup noodle.

我想點一碗雞肉湯麵。

∞ 小提點 ∞

外國人把湯麵定義成有麵的湯，所以他們會說 noodle soup。在國外的中國餐廳的菜單中 Long soup 也是湯麵的意思喔，那猜猜看 short soup 是什麼呢？答案是餛飩湯！一定沒猜到吧！

Dry noodle

【乾麵 Dry noodle】

■ I want to order a dry wonton noodle.
我想要點一碗餛飩乾麵。

【還能怎麼說】

■ One dry noodle with wonton please?
一碗餛飩乾麵。

■ Can I have my wonton noodle dry please?
我的餛飩麵要乾的。

∾ 小提點 ∾

乾麵可以直接用 *dry* 這個字形容。中式乾麵的概念跟西方的 *noodle salad* 麵沙拉是一樣的，都是用拌的。如果要向外國人解釋，這也是不錯的方式。

手搖飲料的添加選擇

★ 情境概述

　　說到搖搖杯（Bubble tea）的添加選擇還真是玲瑯滿目，除了基本款的珍珠（Pearls）之外還有布丁（Pudding）、椰果（Coconut jelly）、蘆薈（Aloe vera）、仙草凍（Grass jelly）而且常常都有新的花樣。除此之外，在國外的手搖飲料店還有很多五顏六色的果凍可以選，我們先來研究這些入門款吧！

情境對話 MP3 003

Toby: I had milk tea before but I prefer something more refreshing, what would you recommend?

Jessica: I think you should try our house special – Tropical fruit tea, it is made with fresh fruit and Earl Grey tea.

Toby: Sounds good. I will have one of those.

Jessica: Sure, what topping would you like?

Toby: I will have coconut jelly, thanks.

托　比：我有試過奶茶，可是我比較喜歡清爽一點的，你有什麼推薦的？

潔西卡：我會推薦你試一下我們的最出名的飲料-熱帶水果茶，是用新鮮水果搭配伯爵茶調製的。

托　比：好啊，那就來一杯吧。

潔西卡：沒問題，那你想加什麼呢？

托　比：加椰果好了，謝謝。

Pearls

【珍珠 Pearls】
- Do you want to add pearls in your drink?

  你的飲料想加珍珠嗎?

··

【還能怎麼說】
- Any pearls for you?

  要加珍珠嗎?

- Any toppings? We have pearls and coffee jelly.

  要加什麼嗎? 我們有珍珠跟咖啡凍可以選擇。

··

✐ 小提點 ✐

珍珠在英文裡可以直譯成 Pearl. 是最受歡的 topping 中的一種。Topping 的意思是指外加的東西,有加上這個東西會就變得更美味的意思。

Cream on top

【cream on top 加奶油】

■ Our coffee with cream on top is very popular.

我們的冰咖啡加奶油很受歡迎。

【還能怎麼說】

■ May I suggest you to try our coffee with cream on top?

我會建議你試試看我們的咖啡加鮮奶油。

■ Coffee with cream on top is highly recommended.

鮮奶油咖啡很受歡迎喔！

∽ 小提點 ∽

外國人比較熟悉的 *topping* 大概就是在咖啡上加上鮮奶油或是冰淇淋和果醬之類的，這些也可以歸類於 *Topping* 喔！

火鍋料

★ 情境概述

　　台灣人超愛吃火鍋，可是火鍋英文到底怎麼講，有人說 Hot Pot，也有人說 Steamboat，或是用日語 Shabu Shabu（涮涮鍋）來表達，其實這些都通用喔！火鍋料最簡單的表達方式就是以原料及作法來區分，例如貢丸就是 Pork ball，蝦漿就是 Shrimp paste / Prawn paste，蛋餃就是 Egg dumpling，豆皮就是 Tofu skin。

Part
01
圖解實用短句篇

Part
02
即時應答篇

情境對話　MP3 004

Joseph: So, what is included in the set menu?

Tracey: You can choose the type of meat that you want, and all set menus come with pork ball, fish dumpling, fish ball, duck blood rice cake, mushrooms and vegetables. There are three soup bases to choose from we have original, Korean Kim Chi flavor and Chinese herbal soup.

Joseph: Alright, I will have the beef set menu with Korean Kim Chi.

喬瑟夫：請問套餐裡面有包含什麼？

崔　西：你可以選擇你想要的肉品，所有的套餐都有貢丸、魚餃、鴨血、香菇還有青菜。有三種湯底可以選擇原味、韓式泡菜口味或是藥膳湯。

喬瑟夫：好，那我要牛肉泡菜鍋。

Extras

餐飲加油站

【額外加點 Extras】

■ If you would like to order extras, here is the price list.

如果你要額外加點的話，價格表在這裡。

- -

【還能怎麼說】

■ You can order extra meat or other items.

你可以另外加點肉或是其他們菜色。

■ If it is not enough for you, you can order extras.

如果不夠的話，你可以額外單點。

❧ 小提點 ❧

有的外國人對火鍋並不熟悉，除了需要跟他們介紹火鍋料之外，他們對食用的方式也可能有疑問，記得要提醒他們還有醬料（Dipping sauce）區喔！

Soup base

【湯底 Soup base】

■ There are three soup base to choose from.

有三種湯底可以選。

【還能怎麼說】

■ We have three different soup base.

我們有三種湯底。

■ Which soup base do you prefer?

你想要哪一種湯底？

∾ 小提點 ∾

大多數外國人對藥膳湯底（Chinese herbal soup）都不會感興趣。如果他們沒主見需要請店家推薦的話，那就直接給他們原味 Original 的吧！

飲品甜度

★ 情境概述

　　對於甜度的選擇不僅在手搖飲料可以用得上，在國外的咖啡店很多也會客製化甜度，只是不像手搖飲料分得這麼細。手搖飲料有正常糖 Standard、半糖 Half sugar、微糖 Little sugar、無糖 No sugar。咖啡的話就是分幾匙糖，正常糖就是一匙 One sugar，喜歡甜一點的大概都是 Two sugar.

情境對話 MP3 005

Alan: I heard they have the best cupcakes in town, can you bring one back for me and also a latte please?

Joy: Sure, what size do you want?

Alan: A large one please.

Joy: Ok, do you take any sugar?

Alan: Yes, just one. How much do I owe you?

Joy: Don't worry. It will be my treat.

阿倫：聽說那家的杯子蛋糕遠近馳名，可以幫我買一個回來，順便在幫我外帶一杯拿鐵好嗎？

喬伊：好啊，你咖啡要大杯小杯？

阿倫：要大杯的，謝謝。

喬伊：那要加糖嗎？

阿倫：要，一匙糖就好。這樣要給你多少錢？

喬伊：不用啦，算我請你。

Standard

【正常甜度 Standard】

■ Most people prefer our milk tea with standard sugar.

大部分的人喜歡我們正常甜度的奶茶。

【還能怎麼說】

■ Our milk tea with standard sugar is the best seller.

我們正常甜度的奶茶賣得很好。

■ Our customer likes our milk tea with normal sugar.

我們的客人最喜歡正常甜度的奶茶。

⤳ 小提點 ⤳

一般人一想到正常就會用 *normal* 這個字，*normal* 也是可以表達出正常甜度的意思，但是用 *standard*（標準）會更貼切喔！

Part
01
圖解實用短句篇

Part
02
即時應答篇

no sugar/ zero sugar
without sugar

【無糖 sugar】

■ Can I have my green tea with no sugar please?

我要一杯無糖綠茶?

【還能怎麼說】

■ One green tea with no sugar please.

一杯無糖綠茶。

■ One green tea please, I don't want any sugar.

我要一杯綠茶,不要加糖。

⚘ 小提點 ⚘

不要糖可以用直譯的方式就是 *No sugar*, 也可以用 *without sugar* 來表示,或是用 *Zero sugar*(零甜度)來說喔!

中式餐具

★ 情境概述

中式餐具是我們一天三餐都需要用到的餐具，與西式餐具最不同的就是筷子（Chopsticks），公筷又叫做 communal（共用的）chopsticks。中式圓桌中間放食物的轉盤有個意想不到的英文名稱叫懶惰的蘇珊（Lazy Susan），合菜常見的餐具還有飯碗（Bowl）、碟子（Plate），還有裝醬料的小碟子（Sauce dish）。

🍴 **情境對話** MP3 006

Jonathan: Excuse me, can we add another dinning set please? There will be 5 of us.

Alice: Not a problem, I will set the table for you.

Jonathan: Thanks, and what is the reason for two sets of chopsticks?

Alice: The black set is the communal one which you use to pick up the food from the center of the table to your bowl. Then you change into the white ones for eating.

- -

強納森：不好意思，可以幫我們加一組餐具嗎？我們一共五個人。

艾莉絲：沒問題，我幫你加餐具。

強納森：謝謝，請問為什麼會有兩組筷子呢？

艾莉絲：黑色的那組是公筷，是用來夾菜到碗裡的，然後再換成白色那組來吃飯。

Dinning set

【餐具 dinning set】

■ Can you add another dinning set for us please?

可以幫我們加餐具嗎？

....

【還能怎麼說】

■ We need extra bowl and chopsticks please.

我們需要多一個碗還有筷子。

■ We got one more person coming, there is not enough bowl and chopsticks.

等一下來有一個人要來，碗跟筷子不夠。

....

☙ **小提點** ☙

跟服務生反應人數的問題也是對的請他依照人數加餐具的意思，如果沒有辦法直接講出 *dinning set* 的話，這樣旁敲側擊服務生也會懂。

Communal chopsticks

【公筷 Communal chopsticks】

■ Do you provide communal chopsticks?

你們有提供公筷嗎？

【還能怎麼說】

■ One more set of chopsticks please?

請多給我們一雙筷子。

■ Please give us extra pair of chopsticks.

請多給我們一雙筷子。

❧ **小提點** ❧

外國人也有公筷母匙的觀念，例如夾取沙拉使用的大湯匙叫做 Serving spoon. 而且在國外如果要沾醬的話，也只能在食物未放入嘴巴之前沾一次，咬過的食物是不可以再沾第二次醬的，不然就犯了所謂 Double dipping（沾兩次）的大忌！

UNIT 7

西式餐具

★ 情境概述

　　西式餐具種類繁多，可以大致上大概分為刀（Knife）、叉（Fork）及湯匙（Spoon）三類，又因為功能性的不同分為前菜（Entrée）的餐具，主菜（Main）的餐具還有甜點湯匙（Dessert spoon），例如前菜叉就叫做 Entrée fork。另外拿來塗奶油的刀子就叫奶油刀（Butter knife），如果點牛排的話通常會附上鋸齒狀的牛排刀（Steak knife）。

🍴 **情境對話** MP3 007

Holly: May I take your order?

Lucas: Sure you may. I will have a Steak sandwich and a small Greek salad.

Holly: Would you like any Entrée? Our deep-fried pork parcel is very popular.

Lucas: No, thanks. I am not hungry today.

Holly: Not a problem, I will bring you a steak knife for your burger.

. . . .

荷　莉：準備好要點餐了嗎？

路卡斯：可以了，我想要一份牛排三明治還有一份小的希臘沙拉。

荷　莉：要不要來份開胃菜?我們的炸豬肉酥餅賣得很好喔！

路卡斯：不用了，謝謝，我今天不太餓。

荷　莉：那沒問題，我待會幫您送上牛排刀。

Steak knife

【牛排刀 **Steak knife**】

■ Can I have a steak knife please? I got a steak coming.

可以給我牛排刀嗎？我點了牛排。

．．．．．．．．．．．．．．．．．．．．．．．．．．．．．．

【還能怎麼說】

■ Can you bring me a steak knife please?

可以幫我送上牛排刀嗎？

■ This knife is too blunt, can I get a steak knife instead?

這把刀太鈍了，可以給我一支牛排刀嗎？

．．．．．．．．．．．．．．．．．．．．．．．．．．．．．．

～ 小提點 ～

牛排刀顧名思義就是設計給切牛排專用的，通常很尖銳，有鋸齒狀，通常不是一般餐具的基本配備，如果需要的話記得要跟服務生特別要求。

Fork

【叉子 Fork】

■ Can you replace the fork for me? It is dirty.

可以幫我換根叉子嗎？這很髒。

【還能怎麼說】

■ Please change the fork for me, it is not clean

請幫我換叉子，這沒洗乾淨。

■ A new fork please, there is something on it.

麻煩給我新的叉子，上面有東西。

❧ 小提點 ❧

叉子是西餐裡不可或缺的餐具，但是通常是主餐才會用上。
台灣人習慣用叉子吃甜點，可是外國人習慣用湯匙吃甜點，
所以才會有 Dessert spoon（甜點匙）的稱號。

飲品相關餐具

★ 情境概述

飲品相關的餐具最常見的就是吸管（Straw），如果是在餐廳內飲用，水杯通常是玻璃杯（Glass），熱飲則會用瓷杯（Cup），另外還會附上糖罐（Sugar jar）。有的餐廳會送上一壺水（A jug of water），如果是外帶的話則需要外帶杯(Takeaway cup）還有外帶用的塑膠袋或紙袋（Carry bag）。

🍴 情境對話　MP3 008

Amanda: Hi, I can't finish my salad, can I have it takeaway please?

Mark: Of course, do you want an extra tub of dressing?

Amanda: Oh, thanks, that will be great.

Mark: Do you need a carry bag?

Amanda: No, thanks. I got a reusable bag and don't worry about cutlery either.

亞曼達：不好意思，我的沙拉吃不完，可以帶走嗎？

馬　克：當然可以，你要不要多一份沙拉醬？

亞曼達：喔，好的，謝謝。

馬　克：你需要塑膠袋嗎？

亞曼達：不用謝謝，我有環保袋，還有，餐具也不需要喔。

餐飲加油站

Takeaway

【外帶 Takeaway】

■ Can I have my ice tea takeaway please?

麻煩你冰紅茶外帶好嗎？

. . . .

【還能怎麼說】

■ Can I have a takeaway cup please.

可以給我一個外帶杯嗎？

■ Ice tea to go please.

冰紅茶外帶。

. . . .

❧ 小提點 ❧

喝不完的東西想外帶除了用 Takeaway 及 To go 來表示之外，最直接的就是跟店家要個外帶杯或是外帶盒之類的，既清楚又明白。

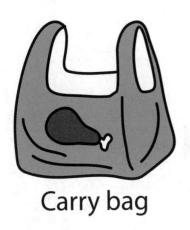

Carry bag

【提袋 **Carry bag**】

■ Please give me a carry bag.
請給我一個提袋。

- -

【還能怎麼說】

■ I need a carry bag as well.
我還需要一個提袋。

■ One carry bag for me please.
請給我一個提袋。

- -

❧ 小提點 ❧

現在環保意識高漲，很多商店都需要付錢買塑膠提袋，所以店家不見得會主動提供紙袋。這種情況下很多人都會自備環保提袋（*Reusable bag*），不但環保又省錢。

附餐飲料

★ 情境概述

在台灣幾乎每間餐廳都會有所謂的套餐組合，最基本的都會有主餐附飲料。附餐飲料的選擇大概有果汁、汽水、咖啡和奶茶等等，有些餐廳還可以加價升級到其他的飲品。附餐飲料基本上可以選擇是隨餐出還是餐後出，就讓我們學學怎麼說吧！

🍴 情境對話 MP3 009

Sophia: What would you like for your drink?

James: What are my choices?

Sophia: You can have juice, soft drink or ice coffee.

James: What juice do you have?

Sophia: We only have apple juice

James: OK, in that case I will have ice coffee, please.

Sophia: Would you like it with or after your meal

James: I will have it with my meal please.

蘇菲亞：請問您飲料要什麼？

詹姆士：請問有什麼可以選？

蘇菲亞：有果汁，汽水或是冰咖啡。

詹姆士：好，那我要冰咖啡好了。

蘇菲亞：請問你要隨餐還是要餐後出？

詹姆士：請幫我隨餐出。

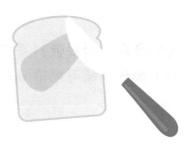

餐飲加油站

【鮮果汁 fresh juice】

■ Can I upgrade to fresh juice please?

可以加價換成鮮果汁嗎？

【還能怎麼說】

■ How much is it to upgrade to fresh juice?

換成鮮果汁要加多少錢？

Fresh juice

■ Is it bottled juice or fresh juice? Can I choose fresh juice?

果汁是罐裝的還是現打的?可以選鮮果汁嗎？

∽ 小提點 ∽

有的餐廳的附餐飲料是固定的，有些則可以加價換成其他飲料，加價換購可以用 upgrade（升等、升級）這個字喔！

Soft drink

【汽水 Soft drink】

■ Can I refill the soft drink?
　汽水可以續杯嗎？

【還能怎麼說】

■ Is the soft drink unlimited?
　汽水是無限暢飲的嗎？

■ What kind of fizzy drink do you have?
　你們有那些氣泡飲料？

∽ 小提點 ∽

汽水的英文是軟性飲料（Soft drink），可以說 Fizzy drink（有氣泡的飲料）。有些餐廳汽水的會是可以續杯的，可以用 Refill（重新裝填）來表達。

咖啡

★ 情境概述

　　咖啡不管是在國內外都是非常受歡迎的飲品，尤其是對外國人來說更是咖啡不離手，就像台灣人愛珍珠奶茶的程度。在台灣冰咖啡的選項很多，如果在國外點冰咖啡，通常是像甜點一樣，把冰淇淋浸在咖啡中，上面再擠上漂亮的奶油擠花，看起來非常的豪華。

🎧 **情境對話** MP3 010

Mandy: Hi, just wondering what is your specialty here?

Chris: Would like to try our ice coffee? We used fresh cream from New Zealand.

Mandy: No, thanks. I am not a big fan of creamy drinks.

Chris: In that case, I will recommend our expresso, we use Brazilian coffee beans.

Mandy: Sounds good. I like a strong one, can I have double expresso please?

曼　蒂：您好，請問你們的招牌是什麼？

克里斯：要不要試試我們的冰咖啡，我們是用紐西蘭進口的鮮奶油。

曼　蒂：還是不要好了，我不喜歡奶味太重的飲料。

克里斯：那這樣的話，我會推薦義式咖啡，我們用的是巴西的咖啡豆。

曼　蒂：那好，我喜歡濃一點的，可以做兩倍濃的義式咖啡嗎？

Strong

【濃 strong】

■ Can you make it stronger?
可以濃一點嗎?

・・

【還能怎麼說】

■ This is too strong for me, can you add more water please?
我喜歡不要那麼濃,可以幫我多加點水嗎?

■ Can I order a weak latte please?
要一杯淡拿鐵。

・・

❧ 小提點 ❧

國外點咖啡時可以指定濃度,通常要濃一點的就是用 Double(兩倍),如果要淡一點的可以用 Weak(淡／虛弱)這個字。淡咖啡還可以指定要 1/2(Half)濃度還是 1/4(Quarter)的超淡咖啡喔。

Creamy

【奶味 Creamy】

■ I like a creamy drink.
我喜歡奶味重的飲料。

……………………………………

【還能怎麼說】

■ Please give me extra cream in my coffee.
請在我的咖啡裡加多一點的奶油。

■ Can I have double cream please.
我要雙倍奶油。

……………………………………

❧ 小提點 ❧

在很多時候，在名詞後面加上 ㄚ 就可以變成形容詞。例如 Cream （奶油）Creamy 就是奶味的意思。Spice （香料／辣椒）Spicy 就變成很辣的意思；Ice（冰）去 e 加上 y 就是 Icy 很多冰，很涼的意思喔。

酒類

　　中文的酒類就包含了所有的酒，可是英文
就可以分很多種。例如伏特加、白蘭地這種叫
烈酒（Spirit），台灣的高粱也可以這麼說。
所謂的紅酒、白酒就是葡萄酒，這種叫做
（Wine），另外一大類就是啤酒了
（Beer）、淡啤酒叫做 Light beer，不是像
咖啡一樣用 Weak 喔。

情境對話　MP3 011

Dylan:　I am going to the shops, do you want anything?

Joe:　What are you getting?

Dylan:　I am just going to get a 6 pack.

Joe:　Can you get a bottle of wine for me please? I am taking it to Doug's house.

Dylan:　What kind of wine?

Joe:　Just any white wine that is on special.

狄倫：我要去買東西，要不要幫你買什麼？

喬：　你要買什麼？

狄倫：我要去買一手啤酒。

喬：　可以幫我買一瓶酒嗎？我要帶去道格家的。

狄倫：好啊，哪一種酒？

喬：　只要是在打折的白酒都可以。

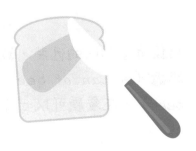

6 pack

【啤酒的數量單位 **6 pack**】

■ We will get a 6 pack.
我們要一手啤酒（6 瓶）。

....

【還能怎麼說】

■ Can we have a jug of beer please?
可以點一壺啤酒嗎？

■ I would like a glass of beer.
我要點一杯啤酒。

....

❧ 小提點 ❧

根據啤酒不同的包裝，數量單位也跟著變化喔。最常見的是鋁罐（A can of beer）不然就是玻璃瓶（A bottle of beer），在餐廳可以一杯一杯點，或是一壺喔。

On special

【特價 on special】

■ The white wine is on special
白酒在特價喔。

- -

【還能怎麼說】

■ The white wine is on sale.
白酒有促銷喔。

■ There is a promotion for white wine.
白酒有特價活動喔。

- -

✎ 小提點 ✎

特價的方式有很多，例如買一送一可以用 *Buy one and get one free*，或是 *Two for the price of one*（兩個算一個的錢），打折的話記得打七折是 *30% off*，不是 *70% off*（打三折）喔！

開胃菜

★ 情境概述

西式的開胃菜（Appetizer）大多都是冷盤，例如燻鮭魚（Smoke salmon），鮮蝦沙拉（Shrimp cocktail）、鵝肝醬（Pate）、火腿片（Ham）等等。中式的開胃菜也都是冷的涼拌菜之類例如：醃黃瓜（Pickle cucumber）、泡菜（Kimchi）、豆干（Dry tofu），毛豆（Edamame beans）等等。開胃菜的份量通常都很少，大概都只有一兩口的量。

情境對話 MP3 012

Tony: Excuse me, what is this dish?

Melissa: That's dry tofu stir fried with dry fish and chili.

Tony: Is it very spicy?

Melissa: No, the chili is just a decoration; it is not spicy at all. But if you really worry about chili, why don't you try the pickle cucumber.

Tony: Sure, it looks good.

東　尼：請問這道菜是什麼？

瑪莉莎：這是辣椒小魚乾炒豆干

東　尼：會很辣嗎？

瑪莉莎：不會，辣椒只是裝飾，一點都不辣。可是你如果不喜歡辣椒的話，那要不要試試看醃黃瓜？

東　尼：好啊，看起來很好吃。

餐飲加油站

Platter

【綜合前菜盤 Platter】

■ The combination cheese platter looks good!

綜合起司盤看起來很好吃。

....

【還能怎麼說】

■ We should order cheese platter as an appetizer.

我們應該點起司盤來當前菜！

■ Do you want to order cheese platter to share?

我們點一個起司盤一起吃好嗎？

....

❧ 小提點 ❧

所謂的 platter 通常是指一大盤讓大家一起吃的菜，起司盤（Cheese platter）是最常見的。還有 Antipasto platter（義式開胃菜盤）也都是很受歡迎的。

Spicy

【辣度 **Spicy**】

■ This Ma Po tofu is too spicy for me.

這道麻婆豆腐對我來說真的太辣了

【還能怎麼說】

■ Can you put less chili in this Ma Po tofu?

麻婆豆腐可以少放點辣嗎？

■ Can you make my Ma Po tofu mild please?

麻婆豆腐可以做微辣就好了嗎？

❧ 小提點 ❧

大部分的菜辣度都可以做調整，要加辣的話就是 *extra spicy*，不要那麼辣就是 *Less spicy*，微辣的話可以用 *Mild* （溫和的）來形容，要不辣的話也可以說 *No Chili*。

認識中式餐點－早餐

★ 情境概述

中式的早餐玲瑯滿目，外國人常常是有看沒有懂，有一些常見的大家一定要知道，例如煎餃 Pan Dried dumpling 或是 pot sticker（鍋貼）、蘿蔔糕 Radish cake、蛋餅 Omelet cake、饅頭（Man Tou / steam bread）、肉包 Pork bun、蔥油餅 Spring onion、燒餅油條（Fried bread and Chinese pastry）、豆漿 Soy milk。

🍴 情境對話　MP3 013

Annie: Wow, there are so many different buns, what's in them?

Terry: The one with black sesame on top is the pork bun, the flat one is leek and pork with glass noodles. The one with nothing on top is the sweet one. It has red bean paste inside.

Annie: Ok, I think I will try the savory one. Can I have the pork bun please?

安妮：哇，有好多種包子喔，這些裡面是包什麼餡料？

泰瑞：上面有黑芝麻的是肉包，扁扁的那種是包韭菜，豬肉還有冬粉。上面沒有撒東西的是甜的，是紅豆餡。

安妮：好的，那我想試試看鹹的。麻煩妳一個肉包。

餐飲加油站

【鹹點 Savory food】

■ I will have a savory pastry please.
我要一個鹹派。

【還能怎麼說】

■ I want to have a pastry with meat.
我想要包肉的那種派。

Savory food

■ Can I have a not sweet one? I don't like sweet pastry.
我想要一個不甜的派，我不喜歡吃甜的。

❧ 小提點 ❧

一般人如果要表達鹹這個字，第一個想到的單字就是 Salt（鹽），然而 Salty 卻是說東西很鹹的意思，並不是口味上的鹹甜，所以要記得所謂鹹點要用 Savory 這個字表達喔！

Stuffing

【內餡 Stuffing】

■ What is the stuffing in this dumpling?

這個水餃內餡是什麼？

- - - - - - - - - - - - - - - - -

【還能怎麼說】

■ What's inside the dumpling?

裡面包什麼？

■ What is this dumpling made with?

這是什麼做的？

· ·

❧ 小提點 ❧

要表達內餡最容易的字就是 Inside（裡面），就跟中文裡說裡面是什麼的意思是一樣的。如果對方解釋了，但卻聽不懂到底是什麼，可以問是 Savory or sweet？至少可以分出是甜的還是鹹的！

認識中式餐點 – 台菜

★ 情境概述

　　要介紹台菜可以從烹調的方式下手，基本上有煎 Pan fry 、蒸 Steam、燉 Slow cook、炒 Stir fry、 油炸 Deep fry、慢燉 Stew、芡汁 Thick sauce 等等。表達菜名的大原則就是烹煮方式或是醬汁口味加上食材就可以，例如 Beef with tomato sauce. 就是茄汁牛肉; Stir fried cabbage 就是炒高麗菜; 羊肉燴飯就是 Stir fried lamb on rice with thick sauce.

Part 01 圖解實用短句篇

Part 02 即時應答篇

情境對話 MP3 014

George: I really like fish, can you recommend a famous fish dish please?

Emma: Sure, do you prefer whole fish or fish fillet?

George: I prefer fish fillet.

Emma: If you like strong flavor, I will recommend you to try our Tariyaki fish. If you prefer something light, our Stir fried celery and fish fillet is also very popular.

喬治：我很喜歡吃魚，可以幫我推薦一道有名的料理嗎？

艾瑪：當然，你喜歡全魚還是魚柳？

喬治：我喜歡魚柳。

艾瑪：如果你喜歡重口味的，我會推薦照燒魚排，如果想吃清淡一點的，那我們的西芹魚片也很棒喔！

Fillet

【無骨肉排 Fillet】

■ I don't like bones, do you have fish fillet?

我不喜歡骨頭，你們有沒有魚排。

....

【還能怎麼說】

■ I like boneless fish, can you fillet it for me?

我喜歡無骨的魚肉，可以幫我去骨嗎？

■ Can you debone the fish and cut the meat out?

可以幫我去骨然後把肉切下來嗎？

....

❧ 小提點 ❧

大部分的外國人都習慣吃魚排，無骨的魚肉依尺寸和加工方式有不同的名稱，一整片的魚排叫 *Fillet*，一些小一點像雞塊整塊的魚肉叫 *Fish nugget*，還有切成條狀裹粉下去炸的魚條叫 *fish finger*。

Fry

【油炸方式 fry】

■ My favorite food is deep fried pork chop.

我最喜歡的就是炸排骨。

【還能怎麼說】

■ I prefer my pork chop deep fried, not pan fried.

我比較喜歡炸排骨，煎得不好吃。

■ If you only have pan fried pork chop, I will order something else.

如果你只有煎排骨的話，那我就點別的。

❧ 小提點 ❧

Fry 這個字除了 Deep fry 還有 Pan fry 之外還有一種叫 Shallow fry 意思就是半煎半炸。就像 Stir fry 是炒的意思，那如果是用涼拌的方式就稱為 Stir through。同樣都是炸跟炒，只是程度不同。

認識中式餐點－小吃

　　台灣庶民的美食文化裡，小吃是一定不能放過的。很多小吃都跟節慶有關，例如肉粽（Rice dumpling）、春捲（Spring roll），其他常見的小吃還有類似滷味（Stew food）、黑輪（Fish cake）、鴨血（Duck blood）、米糕（Sticky rice）、蚵仔煎（Oyster pan cake）。鹽酥雞的話可以稱為（Chicken and chips）因為很類似國外賣炸魚薯條（Fish and chips）的那種店。

情境對話   MP3 015

Marco: What is your favorite Taiwanese food?

Rosie: I would say the pig stomach and pickle soup. Have you tried that before?

Marco: No, but I don't think I will. It sounds a bit scary.

Rosie: It is not scary at all, the pig stomach is very tender but also a little chewy. It is very nice.

馬可：你最喜歡台灣的食物是什麼？

蘿絲：我最喜歡鹹菜豬肚湯了，你有喝過嗎？

馬可：沒有，可是我覺得我也不會想喝，因為聽起來有點恐怖。

蘿絲：才不恐怖呢！那個豬肚很軟嫩，也還 QQ 的，實在很好吃乁！

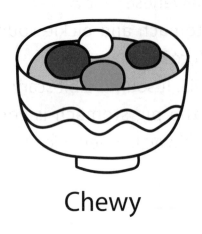

餐飲加油站

【QQ 的 Chewy】

■ I prefer sticky right over white rice, because it is chewy.

跟白飯比較的話，我比較喜歡糯米飯，因為它 QQ 的。

【還能怎麼說】

■ This bit of meat is too chewy, I can't eat.

這塊肉實在咬不動，我沒辦法吃。

■ The texture is not right, it should be more chewy.

這個口感不對，應該是要 QQ 的。

❧ 小提點 ❧

台灣人很喜歡用 Q 來形容口感，與 Q 最對應的英文字應該就是 Chewy 了，就是需要嚼的意思，所以除了可以形容 QQ 的感覺，也可以形容咬不動喔！（因為太 Q 了）

Soup

【羹湯 Soup】

■ Squid in thick soup is a very popular dish in the market.
魷魚羹是很受歡迎的夜市小吃。

【還能怎麼說】

■ People like to eat squid in thick soup in the night market.
大家到夜市都喜歡點魷魚羹。

■ This shop has the best squid in thick soup.
這家的魷魚羹最出名了！

❧ 小提點 ❧

所謂的羹就是溝過濃芡的湯，所以用 *think soup* 就可以輕鬆表達了喔！Soup 這個字不僅僅可以形容鹹的湯品，甜的點心也可以喔，就像紅豆湯就教 *Red bean soup*。

認識西式餐點－主餐

　　西式的主餐可以簡單分成排餐 Steak、義大利麵 Pasta、燉菜 Stew 等等。排餐有豬排（Pork chop）、牛排（Steak）、羊排和魚排。義大利麵通常可以選麵來搭配醬汁，一般常見的麵筆尖麵 Penne、細麵 Angle hair、義大利麵 spaghetti 等等。燉菜（Stew）的話就不外乎紅酒燉牛肉，燉羊膝這類的料理。

🍴 情境對話　MP3 016

Zoe:　What would you like for the main?

Ian:　I can't decide, the lamb shank looks pretty good, but I kind of feel like seafood. What do you recommend?

Zoe:　Our fish of the day is steamed halibut with spring onion sauce. The fish is very tender.

Ian:　I think halibut might be too boney, I think I will go with the lamb shank.

柔伊：請問主餐想要點什麼？

伊恩：很難決定ㄟ，燉洋膝看起來很不錯，可是我又想吃海鮮。

柔伊：我們今天推薦的魚市香蔥蒸鱈魚，魚肉很嫩喔。

伊恩：鱈魚還要挑刺，我看我還是吃羊膝好了。

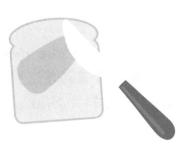

Something of the day

【今日精選 something of the day】

■ The fish of the day is pan fried tuna steak.

今天的特選魚料理是香煎鮪魚排。

【還能怎麼說】

■ The soup of the day is sweet corn soup.

今天的特選濃湯是玉米濃湯。

■ The meal of the day is deep fried pork shop.

今日套餐是炸排骨飯。

❧ 小提點 ❧

Something of the day 可以廣泛利用於介紹餐廳的特選食物，除了今日特餐之外，還可以推薦甜點（Dessert of the day）或飲料（Drink of the day）喔。

Pasta

【義大利麵 Pasta】

- I feel like having pasta today.
  我今天想吃義大利麵ㄟ。

....

【還能怎麼說】

- I know their specialty is steak, but I feel like pasta today.
  我知道這裡的牛排最有名可是我今天比較想吃義大利麵！

- Do you want to do to the pasta house today? I feel like pasta.
  想不想去義大利麵餐廳? 我有點想吃義大利麵。

....

⚘ 小提點 ⚘

Pasta 廣義的義大利麵，不管是筆管麵（Penne），細麵（Angel hair），寬麵（Fettachini）都是 Pasta 的一種。在國外的餐廳些是可以客製化，自己選麵款及醬汁。

認識西式餐點－附餐

★ 情境概述

　　西點的附餐大概可以分成湯品、沙拉和甜點。湯品常會附上蒜味麵包（Garlic bread）。沙拉的話可以選擇不同的種類例如凱薩沙拉或是希臘沙拉之類，有的餐廳則是可以選擇搭配不同的沙拉醬（Dressing），例如千島醬（Thousand island）、和風醬（Japanese），或是意式油醋醬（Italian）。甜點除了蛋糕之外還有焦糖布丁（Creme Brulee）也很常見。

🍴 **情境對話** MP3 017

Candice: For an extra 199NT, you get soup, salad and dessert. Our soup of the day is seafood chowder.

Andrew: Does it come with bread?

Candice: Yes, it does. You get two slices of bread.

Andrew: Ok, I will go for the combo then. Can I have a Cesar salad please?

Candice: Sorry, we only have one type of salad, but you can choose between Japanese dressing or Italian dressing.

凱蒂斯：如果加 199 元就會有湯、沙拉和甜點。我們的今日濃湯是海鮮巧達湯。

安德魯：有附麵包嗎？

凱蒂斯：有，有附兩片麵包。

安德魯：好，那我加套餐好了，可以選凱薩沙拉嗎？

凱蒂斯：抱歉，我們只有一種沙拉，可是你可以選要和風醬還是意式油醋醬。

Salad dressing

【沙拉醬 Salad dressing】

■ The combo includes a salad with Italian dressing.
套餐有附一分義式油醋醬沙拉。

【還能怎麼說】

■ If you order combo, you will have a salad with Italian dressing.
如果你選套餐的話，會有沙拉還會附上義式油醋醬。

■ If you want salad with Italian dressing, you can order combo.
如果你要義士油醋沙拉的話，你可以點套餐。

＆ 小提點 ＆

Dressing 是沙拉醬汁的意思，通常國外的餐廳裡會有多種的 dressing 可供選擇。最常見的除了 Italian dressing（義式油醋醬），還有 French dressing（法式沙拉醬汁）。

Bread

【麵包 bread】

■ You can choose between garlic bread and herb bread.

大蒜麵包或是香料麵包你可以二選一。

- -

【還能怎麼說】

■ If you don't want garlic bread, you can choose herb bread.

如果你不要大蒜麵包的話，那可以選香料麵包。

■ For bread, we have garlic bread and herb bread, you can pick one.

麵包的話我們有大蒜麵包和香料麵包，你可以選一個。

· ·

⤳ 小提點 ⤳

麵包也是西式附餐的一個重點，最常見的麵包除了大蒜麵包 *Garlic bread* 之外，還有香料麵包 *Herb bread*，現在也很流行義式麵包例如佛卡夏等等。

牛排熟度

★ 情境概述

　　點牛排最重要問題就是熟度了，愛吃牛排的饕客相信牛肉越熟的話，肉就越老，所以很少人會點全熟（Well done）。敢吃生的人還可以點 Blue steak（1 分熟），其他比較常見的大概是三分熟（Rare）、五分熟（Medium rare）、七分熟（Medium well）。煎得太熟了就是 Overcooked,不夠熟就是 Underdone。

情境對話　MP3 018

Malinda: If you like steak, our sirloin steak is very popular. You can try it.

Justin: I think I will, I like my steak tender, can you make sure the chef does not overcook it?

Malinda: Sure, I will let the chef know you would like your steak rare.

Justin: I'd rather it underdone than overdone.

瑪琳達：如果你喜歡吃牛排的話，你可以試試我們的沙朗牛排。

賈斯汀：好的，我會。我喜歡吃軟嫩一點的牛排，請你交代廚師不要煎得太熟。

瑪琳達：好的我會跟廚師交代你要三分熟就好。

賈斯汀：我情願生一點，也不要過熟。

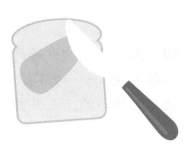

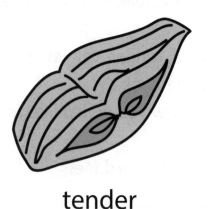

tender

【口感 tender】

■ This steak is very tender, it is cooked perfectly.

這牛排好軟嫩喔，烹煮的恰到好處。

・・・・・・・・・・・・・・・・・・・・・・・・・・・・・・

【還能怎麼說】

■ This steak is perfect, it is not tough at all.

這牛排煎的真好，一點都不硬。

■ This steak is soft and juice, it is very tasty.

這塊牛排又嫩又多汁，實在很好吃。

・・

⤷ 小提點 ⤶

對於肉類口感的形容可以用 Tender 軟嫩，Tough 很硬，咬不動，Stringy 咬不斷。也可以比較肥瘦，例如 Fatty 就是油花比較多的，而外國人都比較喜歡瘦肉 Lean meat。

【熟度的比較 Over, under, just right】

■ This steam fish is a bit underdone.
這條魚沒有蒸熟。

Over, under, just right

【還能怎麼說】

■ This steam fish is a bit overcooked, the meat is too tough.
這條魚蒸過頭了,肉太老了。

■ This steam fish is just right, the meat is very tender.
這魚蒸的剛剛好,肉很嫩。

∽ 小提點 ∾

火侯的拿捏並不是件容易的事,形容煮得剛剛好就是 *Just right!* 過頭就用 *Overcooked* 或 *overdone* 來形容,那不夠的話就是 *Undercooked* 或 *underdone*。

肉類部位

★ 情境概述

　　以牛排來說常見的部位有沙朗 Sirloin、丁骨 T-born、菲力 Fillet、肋眼牛排 Rib eye，或是像王品牛排那種牛肋排 Rib steak。豬肉的話煮湯的那種排骨稱為 Spare ribs，排骨飯的那種整片的排骨稱為 Pork chop，煮義大利麵的絞肉稱為 Mince。大家猜猜五花肉怎麼說，答案是 Pork belly 可別以為是豬肚喔！

情境對話　MP3 019

Tara: There are so many different cuts, I don't know what to choose.

Jimmy: Well, if you prefer lean meat, I will suggest you to try tenderloin. If you prefer something more juicy, then I will recommend pork belly, it is great for BBQ.

Tara: I think pork belly might be a bit too greasy for me. I will try the tenderloin.

塔拉：有好多不同的部位可以許選擇喔，我真不知道怎麼選。

吉米：如果你喜歡瘦一點的，那我建議試試看里肌，如果你喜歡多汁一點的口感，那我建議試試五花肉，烤起來很好吃喔！

塔拉：我覺得五花肉可能太油膩了，我要里肌好了。

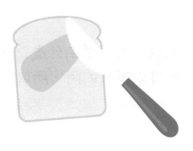

Cuts

【部位 cuts】

■ What is your favorite cut?
你最喜歡吃的部位是哪裡？

....

【還能怎麼說】

■ I like this cut the most.
這是我最喜歡的部位。

■ I always want to try different cut.
我一直都想試試看不同的部位。

....

∽ 小提點 ∽

大家一定在想為什麼 cuts 是部位的意思呢？因為肉都一刀一刀切下來的阿，所以不同的切法就是代表不同的部位。

Chicken Drumstick

【雞腿部位 Chicken Drunstick】

■ I love chicken drum stick the best.
我最喜歡吃雞腿了！

- -

【還能怎麼說】

■ I prefer chicken thigh fillet, it is just right.
我喜歡吃去骨雞腿排，口感剛剛好。

■ I like grilled chicken maryland.
我很喜歡烤的大雞腿。

- -

∽ 小提點 ∽

同樣是雞腿，不同部位有不同的稱呼。棒棒腿叫做 Drum stick（鼓捧），棒棒腿上方的大腿叫 Chicken thigh，棒棒腿跟大腿連在一起的大雞腿則叫 Maryland。

沾醬選擇

★ 情境概述

　　沾醬是個不分中外都很受歡迎的配料，有時候缺了沾醬就會覺得東西不好吃。在國外最受歡迎的沾醬應該就是蕃茄醬（Ketchup）了，當然泰式甜辣醬（Sweet chili sauce）也相當受歡迎。中式的話不外乎就是醬油（Soy sauce）了，辣椒醬（Chili paste）等等。中式的醬料裡常常會加入香油（Sesame oil），薑絲（Ginger），蒜泥（Garlic paste），醋（Vinegar）來調味。

🍴 **情境對話** MP3 020

Polly: Do you need to make your own sauce?

Martin: Yes, I will make a special soy sauce when I have dumplings.

Polly: Ok, can you show me what to do.

Martin: Sure, first of all, you put some sauce soy in, then mix with some vinegar, sugar and a little bit of sesame oil. I will normally put some garlic in it, but some people prefer ginger.

寶麗：我們要自己弄沾醬嗎？

馬丁：是阿，通常吃水餃的時候都會自己調特製醬油。

寶麗：好，那你教我要怎麼弄。

馬丁：當然，你要先倒一點醬油，然後加一點醋，糖然後再加一點香油。有的人會加薑絲，可是我喜歡加蒜泥。

A little of vinegar

【醬料比例：一點點醋】

■ I like to put a little of vinegar into my soy sauce.

我喜歡在醬油裡加點一點點醋。

【還能怎麼說】

■ I like to put half vinegar and half soy sauce when I make a dipping sauce.

我做沾醬的時候喜歡放一半醬油一半的醋。

■ I like to put lots of vinegar in my sauce.

我的醬汁裡喜歡加很多的醋。

∽ 小提點 ∽

調製的比例會直接影響醬料的口味（Taste）。因為醬汁是液體所以如果是要大概倒一點點的話就用 *a little*，如果要明確地說滴幾滴，那就用 *a few drops* 來表示。

Chili sauce on the side

【醬料擺放的位置：辣椒醬放旁邊】

■ Can I have my chili sauce on the side please?

我的辣椒醬可以另外放旁邊嗎？

【還能怎麼說】

■ Can I have the chili sauce on top of the chicken please?

辣椒醬麻煩你幫我加在雞肉上面。

■ Can I have the chili sauce all over the noodles please?

請幫我把麵加很多辣椒醬在上面。

❧ 小提點 ❧

如果是沾醬（Dipping sauce）的話通常是會放在旁邊（On the side），但是如果是淋醬（Gravy）的話，那就可以選擇放旁邊或是直接在食物上面（On top）。

外帶服務

除了所謂的吃到飽（All you can eat）、無限量的自助餐（Buffet）、沙拉吧（Salad bar）之外，大部分的餐點都是可以外帶的。外帶可以用 To go 或是 Takeaway 來表示，到餐廳點餐常常會被問 To go or to have here?（這裡吃還是外帶），這句話除了很實用之外，也很容易記喔！

🍴 **情境對話** MP3 021

Joanna: Hi, I ordered an extra burrito for takeaway. Can you check with the kitchen to see if it is ready?

Darren: Sure, won't be long.

Joanna: And can I have a takeaway container for the leftovers please? I couldn't finish and I don't want it to go to waste.

Darren: Not a problem, I will pack them for you.

喬安娜：您好，我有多點了一個墨西哥捲要外帶，可以幫我看一下好了沒嗎？

戴　倫：沒問題，等我一下。

喬安娜：還有，可以給我個外帶盒嗎？我想把剩下的帶回去,不要浪費。

戴　倫：沒問題，我來幫你包。

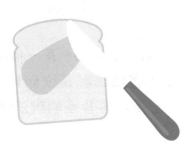

🍎 餐飲加油站

All you can eat

【自助餐 All you can eat】

■ I like to go to Grand hotel for their all you can eat. They have great seafood selection.

我最喜歡去圓山飯店吃自助餐,他們的海鮮種類繁多。

. . . .

【還能怎麼說】

■ Grand hotel is famous for their seafood buffet.

圓山飯店的海鮮自助餐很有名。

■ The buffet in Grand hotel has lots of different seafood.

圓山飯店的自助餐有很多種的海鮮。

. . . .

∾ 小提點 ∾

All you can eat 是一個很有趣的直譯,就是所有的你都可以吃,當然也就是吃到飽自助餐的意思! 在國外 All you can eat 是非常普遍的說法喔!

Leftover

【剩菜 Leftover】

■ We finished the whole pizza, there is no leftover.
我們把比薩全吃光了，一片都不剩。

. . . .

【還能怎麼說】

■ The pizza is all gone, nothing left.
比薩都吃光了，什麼都沒剩。

■ There is no leftover pizza.
沒有剩下的比薩了。

. . . .

❧ 小提點 ❧

Leftover 就是剩下的意思，無論是蛋糕吃到剩一片，或是魚吃到剩一口，都是 Leftover 喔！是一個可以廣義表達剩菜的字，非常實用！

催促 / 提醒

★ 情境概述

　　點完菜之後久久不出菜實在是個麻煩的窘境，不提出質問心裡會很不踏實，畢竟餐廳漏單也是常發生。可以說 Excuse me（不好意思）客氣地提醒服務生，請他們（Hurry）快一點，或是再查一查（Check again），這都是很可以接受的喔！

情境對話 MP3 022

Simon: We have been sitting here for at least half an hour, can you please check when our food is coming?

Kristy: I am very sorry, we have very busy today. I will check with the kitchen right away.

Simon: Can you please get them to hurry. We need to get back to work at 1.

∙∙

賽 門：我們已經坐了至少半個小時了，你可以查一下我們的餐點還有多久會好？

克莉絲提：很抱歉我們今天很忙，我現在馬上去幫您看看。

賽 門：請催他快一點，因為我們一點還要回去上班。

餐飲加油站

Wait for a quarter

【15 分鐘 a quarter】

■ We have been waiting here for at least a quarter. The service is very poor.

我們已經等了 15 分鐘了。服務很不好。

· ·

【還能怎麼說】

■ No one came and served us, and we have been standing here for at least half an hour. 我們站了至少 30 分鐘，都沒有人來招呼我們。

■ It is quarter to 1 now, we have been waiting for at least 20 minutes,

現在已經是 12:45 了，我們等了至少 20 分鐘。

· ·

❧ 小提點 ❧

外國人喜歡把 60 分鐘分 4 等分，每 15 分鐘就是一個 Quarter（即 1/4）。如果別人說 Quarter to 1，那就是離 1 點還有 15 分鐘，等同於 12:45 分的意思。

Upset about the service

【生氣、不高興 upset】

■ I am very upset about the service, I have been waiting for over 30 minutes for my meal!
我很生氣，我已經等了 30 分鐘了
餐點還沒來！

【還能怎麼說】

■ I am very upset, I want to speak to the manager; my food is still not here. 我很不高興，請幫我叫經理來，我的餐單到現在還沒來。

■ I want to make a complaint, the meal is taking too long.
我要客訴，餐點實在太慢了。

✎ 小提點 ✎

等到不耐煩的情緒可以用 *Upset* 形容，就是很不高興的意思。不高興避免不了要客訴，除了說要 *make a complaint* 也可以直接跟服務生講叫經理來！

額外付費服務

★ 情境概述

　　某些餐廳尤其是可以辦大型宴會的餐廳可以提供額外的付費服務，例如請樂團來演奏，送花，或是特殊的場地布置或食材等等。外加的服務（Add-ons）可以先向餐廳詢問價格，有的餐廳會有價格表（Price list），如果沒有的話可以請餐廳報價（Quotation）。

情境對話 MP3 023

Zack: I want to organize some music for my girlfriend's birthday party, what kind of options do you have?

Lucy: If you prefer live music we do have a Jazz band, it is 5,000 for 2 hours. Or alternatively you can hire the DJ for the evening and it is 3000.

Zack: Can I bring in my own band?

Lucy: Of course, but we charge 1000 for using the equipment.

查克：我女朋友的生日趴上我想安排音樂，你們有什麼選擇？

露西：如果你要現場表演的話，我們是有個爵士樂團，兩小時要五千塊。如果你想要請 DJ 的話，那 3000 元一個晚上。

查克：那我可以自己找樂團嗎？

露西：當然可以，但是我們酌收 1000 的設備費。

餐飲加油站

List price

【定價 List price】

■ The jazz band will cost you 5000 for two hours. This is the list price.

爵士樂團的收費是 2 個小時 5000 元，這是他們的訂價。

【還能怎麼說】

■ It is 5000 for two hours to hire a Jazz band.

要請爵士樂團的話兩個小時是 5000 元。

■ The list price for the Jazz band is 5000 for two hours.

爵士樂團是 2 個小時 5000 元。

✎ 小提點 ✎

一個小時多少錢用英文的講法要把它反過來想，變成多少錢一個小時，例如 *100 for one hour* 就是一個小時 *100* 元，這樣就很容易記了。

Valet parking

【代客停車 valet parking】

■ Do you have valet parking?
你們有代客停車嗎？

【還能怎麼說】

■ How much do you charge for valet parking?
代客停車要多少錢？

■ Is valet parking for members only?
要會員才能使用代客停車嗎？

❧ 小提點 ❧

有些餐廳或旅館會提供 Valet parking，費用的話可能要先問清楚。如果是免費的情況下，也不要忘了給停車小弟一點小費（Tips）喔。

認識中式甜點

★ 情境概述

中式的甜點有很多都是湯湯水水，例如銀耳蓮子湯（Wood ear and lotus seed soup）、八寶粥（Combination sticky rice porridge）、西米露（Saigo soup），芝麻糊（Sesame paste），也有很多酥餅類，例如鳳梨酥（Pineapple cake）、芋頭酥（Taro cake）、杏仁餅（Almond cookie）或是糕點類例如年糕（Rice cake）、炸元宵（Deep fried sticky rice ball）等等。

🍴 **情境對話** MP3 024

Ashley: I would say my favorite Chinese style desert is the deep fried sticky rice ball.

Thomas: Why is that?

Ashley: it is crispy on the outside and gooey on the inside, it is so yummy. But you've got to watch out when you eat it. Because it is very hot, it could burn your lips.

愛旭麗：我最喜歡的中式甜點就是炸元宵了。

湯瑪士：為什麼呢？

愛旭麗：因為它外酥內軟，超美味的。可是要吃的時候要小心，因為它很燙，可能會燙到嘴。

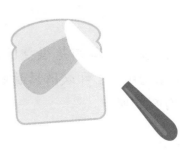

Fried ice cream

【炸冰淇淋 Fried ice bream】

- The skin of this fired ice cream is so crispy. It's my favorite.

  這炸冰淇淋的外皮好脆喔。這是我最喜歡的。

. . . .

【還能怎麼說】

- Fried ice cream is my favorite.

  我最喜歡吃炸冰淇淋了。

- I love the outside of fried ice cream the most. It is so crispy.

  我最喜歡炸冰淇淋的外皮了。它超脆的。

. . . .

⤳ 小提點 ⤳

Crispy 形容的是很薄脆的口感，就如同炸冰淇淋的外皮。
Crunchy 也可以形容脆的口感，但是比較像大口咬下很要用力咬的脆。

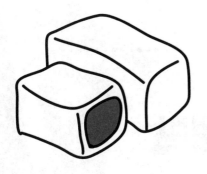

Pineapple cake

【鳳梨酥 Pineapple cake】

■ This pineapple cake is buttery on the outside but sweet on the inside.

這個鳳梨酥外皮很有奶油香,而且裡面很甜。

· ·

【還能怎麼說】

■ The pineapple cake is so taste, the pastry is very buttery. 這個鳳梨酥很美味,外皮有濃濃的奶油香。

■ The pineapple cake is crunchy on the outside but soft on the inside.

這個鳳梨酥真是外酥內軟。

· ·

❧ 小提點 ❧

像鳳梨酥這樣有分內外層的東西,可以用 *On the outside / On the inside* 來分別形容對比的口感,就像外酥內軟,或是外酸內甜等等,對於形容食物的口感來說會很有層次感。

認識西式甜點

★ 情境概述

　　說到西式的甜點，自然就會聯想到起司蛋糕、黑森林蛋糕、蘋果派這類。當然有些像奶酪、果凍等等。國外還有些很受歡迎的品項但在台灣很少見，例如蘿蔔蛋糕、蛋糕主體加入了紅蘿蔔還有核桃及香料，上面附上一層特別的糖霜，糖霜本身是軟的起司做的，口味酸酸甜甜。

情境對話　MP3 025

Ryan: Would you like any dessert? Our daily special is Black forest cake.

Emily: Well, I prefer something else. That apple strudel looks really good, can I have a slice please?

Ryan: Of course, would you like fresh cream and ice cream?

Emily: Just the ice cream will be fine.

Ryan: How many scoops?

Emily: Two please.

萊　恩：需要甜點嗎？我們今天的特製甜點是黑森林蛋糕。

艾蜜莉：嗯，我想點別的，那個蘋果派看起來很棒，可以要一份嗎？

萊　恩：當然可以，你要加鮮奶油還有冰淇淋嗎？

艾蜜莉：只要冰淇淋就好。

萊　恩：那要幾球呢？

艾蜜莉：請給我兩球。

A slice

【蛋糕的數量詞 a slice】

■ Can I have a slice of carrot cake please?

麻煩你一片蘿蔔蛋糕。

. . . .

【還能怎麼說】

■ Can I have some cake please? Just a small piece.

我可以吃一點蛋糕嗎？一小塊就好。

■ Can I have a serve of carrot cake please?

可以點一份蘿蔔蛋糕嗎？

. . . .

◈ 小提點 ◈

到餐廳點蛋糕都是切好一片片賣的，所以要點的時候可以說 A slice（一片）或是 A serve（一份）。如果切成方塊型的，也可以用 A piece（一塊）。

A scoop

【冰淇淋的數量詞 a scoop】

■ Can I have two scoops please?
One Vanilla and one Mango.

可以給我兩球冰淇淋嗎？一球香草的，一球芒果的。

【還能怎麼說】

■ How many scoops of ice cream in one serve?

你們一份冰淇淋有幾球？

■ Can you add one scoop of ice cream on my cake please?

我的蛋糕可以加一球冰淇淋嗎？

❧ 小提點 ❧

一球冰淇淋可不是 one ball 喔，因為冰淇淋是用圓湯匙挖出來的，所以要用 scoop。Scoop 同時也是動詞，是挖出來的意思喔！

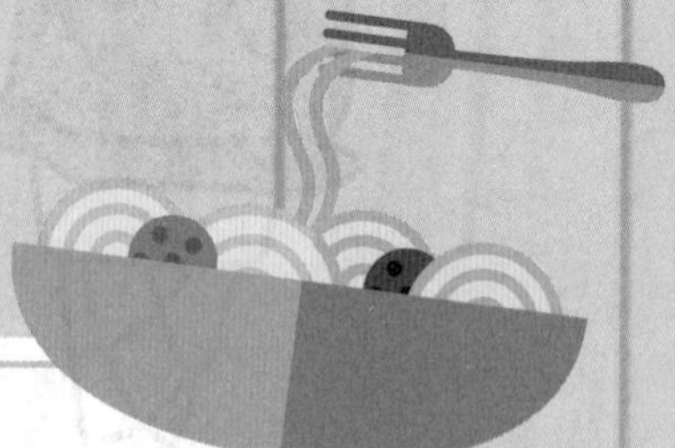

即時應答篇收錄最常使用的餐飲短句，好學易
上手，最短時間內就能學以致用。每單元短句
後更附一問三答單元規劃，三種答法豐富表達
和各式狀況，快跟著書中的句型開始練習吧！

PART 2

·即時應答篇·

飯店訂位和座位

超實用短句 1

❶ 我想要訂位。

⇨ I'd like to make a reservation.

❷ 你們星期五晚上還有空位嗎？

⇨ Are you fully booked this Friday night?

❸ 可以幫我留一張兩個人的桌子嗎？

⇨ Can I have a table for two please?

❹ 我想要靠窗的桌子。

⇨ I would prefer the table by the window.

⚘ 超實用短句 2

❶ 我們一共六個人。

⇨ We are a party of 6.

❷ 需不需要先付訂金？

⇨ Do you require any deposit?

❸ 我們需要兩個兒童高腳餐椅。

⇨ We need two high chairs.

❹ 我不要靠近廁所的位置。

⇨ I prefer somewhere away from the toilet.

MEMO

Q1 Can we have the lounge area?
我們可以坐沙發區嗎？

Audrey Well, our lounge area is quite small, it is designed for a maximum of 4 people, and there are 6 of you, I would suggest the round table, there is more room for everyone.

奧黛莉 嗯，我們的沙發區很小，大概只能坐 4 個人，而你們有六個，我會建議你們坐圓桌，這樣位子比較大。

Sabrina Of course you can. But I need to remind you the table in the lounge area is very low. It is difficult to have meals there.

莎賓娜 當然可以，只是我要提醒您，我們沙發區的桌子很低，如果要吃餐點會不方便。

Dexter　Sorry the lounge area is booked up, but we got a nice outdoor area with big chairs, it is quite nice, too. Do you want me to reserve it for you?

戴斯特　抱歉沙發區已經有預訂了，我們的戶外區也很不錯，椅子大又舒服。要不要預約戶外區？

字彙表

round table	圓桌
lounge area	沙發區
outdoor area	戶外區
booked out	訂滿了

MEMO

🔔 **超實用短句 1**

❶ 我的甜點可以先上嗎？
 ⇨ Can I have my dessert first?

❷ 我的咖啡要跟甜點一起上。
 ⇨ Can I have my coffee with dessert please?

❸ 請幫我上主菜。
 ⇨ I will have my main now.

❹ 我不想點前菜。
 ⇨ I don't want any entrée.

 **超實用短句 2**

❶ 飲料可以幫我隨餐送嗎？
⇨ Can I have my drink with the meal please?

❷ 我的湯可以最後在送嗎？
⇨ Can I have my soup last please?

❸ 我的附餐想跟主菜一起出。
⇨ Can I have the side dish with my main please?

❹ 主菜吃完後可以就上甜點嗎？
⇨ Can I have my dessert right after the main please?

MEMO

Q2 Can I swap a drink for salad?
我的飲料可以換成沙拉嗎？

Audrey   Sure you can, you can pick three out of the four side dishes when you order a value combo. You can have soup, salad plus dessert if you wish.

🔊

奧黛莉   當然可以，當你點超值套餐時，四項附餐選項可以任選三樣。你喜歡的話你可以選湯，沙拉還有甜點。

Sabrina   Unfortunately, it is a set menu, we don't allow any changes. I will suggest you to order a side salad for extra NT50. It is still a very good value.

🔊

莎賓娜   不好意思，這是套餐不能改。我會建議你另外點一個小莎拉，只要加 50 元而已，還是很划算喔!

Dexter   Yes, you can, but there is a NT30 surcharge to make up the difference in price. Would you like a Greek Salad or garden salad?

戴斯特   可以，但是需要多付 30 元的差額，請問你要希臘沙拉還是田園沙拉？

Part
01 圖解實用短句篇

Part
02 即時應答篇

字彙表

value combo	超值套餐
surcharge	差額、費用
side dish	小菜、附餐
extra	額外的、多的

MEMO

🔔 **超實用短句 1**

❶ 不好意思，我改變心意了。

⇨ Sorry, I change my mind.

❷ 我不要炒飯了，我想要牛肉麵。

⇨ Can I have beef noodle instead of fried rice?

❸ 不好意思，我想改一下我的點餐內容。

⇨ Sorry, I want to change my order.

❹ 現在說要取消我的前菜來得及嗎？

⇨ Is it too late to cancel my starter?

🔔 超實用短句 2

❶ 抱歉我忘了跟你說麵裡面不要加辣椒。

⇨ Sorry I forgot to tell you not to put chilly in my noodle.

❷ 我想把主菜從魚換成牛排。

⇨ I want to change my main from fish to steak.

❸ 我點了蘑菇醬，可是我想換成黑胡椒醬，可以嗎？

⇨ I ordered mushroom sauce, but can I change it into pepper sauce please?

❹ 我點了中杯咖啡，現在要改大杯會來的及嗎？

⇨ I ordered a regular coffee, is it too late to upgrade it to a large?

MEMO

Q3 Can I change my main dish to seafood pasta?

我的主菜可以改成海鮮義大利麵嗎？

Audrey Let me check with the kitchen, and I will come back to you. If they haven't started to prepare the dish, then there is no problem.

♪

奧黛莉 讓我問一下廚房，我等一下再跟您確認，通常如果他們還沒開始準備，讓都可以改。

Sabrina Sure you can, I haven't put the order through yet. You can change it now if you wish. Anything else you would like to change?

♪

莎賓娜 當然可以，我還沒把餐點內容送出去，如果要改的話現在可以改，還有其他的東西想改嗎？

Dexter I am sorry. I am afraid the kitchen has already started to prepare the steak, and it is too late to make any changes.

戴斯特 很抱歉廚房恐怕已經開始在準備牛排了,現在來不及做更改了。

🍞 字彙表

I am afraid...	恐怕
if you wish	如果你想要的話
too late to...	來不及...
make changes	更改

MEMO

• UNIT4 •
飯店餐點送錯

超實用短句 1

❶ 我沒點這個。
⇨ I didn't order this.

❷ 這不是我點的餐。
⇨ This is not what I ordered.

❸ 你是不是幫我們點錯了。
⇨ I think you got the order wrong.

❹ 請你再查一下點菜內容。這不是我點的。
⇨ You might want to change the order again. This is not for me.

超實用短句 2

❶ 這應該是別桌的。我們沒有點炸魚薯條。

⇨ This is for a different table. We didn't order fish and chips.

❷ 我點的是素食餐。這一看就知道不是我的。

⇨ I ordered a vegetarian meal. This is the wrong order.

❸ 可以在幫我查一下點餐內容嗎？我很確定我有點炒飯。

⇨ Can you check the order again please? I am pretty sure I ordered a fried rice.

❹ 我點的是糖醋排骨餐，可是這是辣味排骨。

⇨ I ordered a sweet and sour pork meal, but this is chilly pork.

Q4 Excuse me, this is not what I ordered.
抱歉，這不是我點的。

Audrey　Really? Let me check the order again for you, you ordered a large Hainanese chicken rice and soup. This is the right order.

奧黛莉　真的嗎？讓我看一下點餐內容，你點的是大的海南雞飯附湯。這個沒有錯啊。

Sabrina　Oh, Let me check again. Yes, you are right. I am sorry I think the kitchen got the order wrong, I will get them to make yours one right away.

莎賓娜　喔！這樣嗎，讓我看一下。真的對不起，廚房做錯了，我馬上請廚房準備你的餐點。

Dexter　I am sorry, I got the table number wrong. This is actually for the table next to you, your order won't be too long now.

🔔

戴斯特　對不起我看錯桌號。這是要給你隔壁桌的，你的餐點馬上來。

🍞 字彙表

got it wrong	搞錯了
right away	即刻
won't be long	馬上來
next to	在某物的旁邊

MEMO

飯店訂房

🔔 超實用短句 1

❶ 我可以只點主餐嗎？

⇨ Can I order just the main?

❷ 有套餐嗎？

⇨ Do you have set menu?

❸ 我們可以只點一份餐嗎？

⇨ Can we share a meal?

❹ 有沒有個人低消？

⇨ Is there a minimum charge per person?

超實用短句 2

❶ 一定要點飲料嗎？

⇨ Do I have to order a drink?

❷ 飲料可以續杯嗎？

⇨ Can I refill the drink?

❸ 自助餐多少錢？

⇨ How much is for the buffet?

❹ 有沒有附湯？

⇨ Does it come with soup?

MEMO

Q5 Can we do A la carte?
可以單點嗎？

Audrey Certainly, we have a wide range of items available for A la carte. However, I would recommend the set menu because it is a much better value for the money.

奧黛莉 當然可以，我們有很多單點的選項。可是我會建議您點套餐，因為比較划算。

Sabrina I am sorry we do not serve A la carte on the weekends. We only do all-you-can-eat seafood buffet for 1000 per person plus a 10% service charge.

莎賓娜 很抱歉我們周末不提供單點。我們只有海鮮自助餐吃到飽，一個人一千塊，外加一成服務費。

Dexter Yes, of course. You can order just the main meal and add side dishes or soup if you wish. You don't have to order the set menu. The soft drink is free if you order any main meal.

戴斯特 當然可以，你可以只點主餐，或是要外加小菜還是湯品也可以，不是一定要點套餐。如果有點主餐的話我們有提供免費汽水。

字彙表

A la carte	單點
Set menu	套餐
All-you-can-eat	吃到飽
Main meal	主菜

MEMO

飯店食材詢問

🔔 超實用短句 1

❶ 你們有和牛嗎？

⇨ Do you have Wagyu beef?

❷ 你們秋天有供應螃蟹嗎？

⇨ Do you offer crabs in autumn?

❸ 我最喜歡新鮮的菜了，你們有什麼種類的蔬菜？

⇨ I love fresh vegetables, what vegetables do you have?

❹ 有哪些種類的麵包可供選擇？

⇨ What are your selections in terms of bread?

🔔 超實用短句 2

❶ 這個季節有什麼水果？

⇨ What kind of fruit is in season?

❷ 你們有那些肉可供選擇？

⇨ What sort of meat do you have?

❸ 請問烤魚下巴也是自助餐的菜色之一嗎？

⇨ Is BBQ fish jaw part of the buffet selections?

❹ 感恩節的時候你們有賣火雞嗎？

⇨ Do you sell turkey for thanksgiving?

MEMO

Q6 What are the selections of your buffet?
你們的自助餐有什麼菜色？

Audrey We have a very nice carvery section if you like roast beef and ham. We also got a wide range of seafood; crabs are in season which are very tasty.

奧黛莉　我們的現切烤肉區有很棒的烤牛肉還有火腿，我們還有多種的海鮮，尤其是螃蟹現在正是肥美。

Sabrina There are 4 sections; we have a Japanese food section with cold food and sashimi. Hot food section and also a salad bar and dessert bar.

莎賓娜　我們一共分四區，日式餐點區有冷盤還有生魚片，還有熟食區，沙拉區以及甜點區。

Dexter In the Western food area we have Pizza and made-to-order pasta, and in the Asian food area there are 8 different hot dishes.

戴斯特 西餐區我們有披薩還有現點現煮的義大利麵，亞洲區的話由八道不同的熟食。

字彙表

carvery	現切大塊烤肉
hot food	熟食
cold food	冷盤
made-to-order	現點現做

飯店素食

🔔 超實用短句 1

❶ 你們有賣素食嗎？

⇨ Do you have vegetarian food?

❷ 素食有什麼選擇？

⇨ What kind of vegetarian food do you have?

❸ 你們有素食的菜單嗎？

⇨ Where is your vegetarian food menu?

❹ 我菜裡面請不要放動物油。

⇨ Can you not put animal fat in my order please?

超實用短句 2

❶ 我的菜裡面請不要加大蒜還有洋蔥。

⇨ Please don't put garlic and onion in my order.

❷ 我只吃素食。

⇨ I follow a strict vegetarian diet.

❸ 你們有專門給素食者的餐點嗎？

⇨ Do you cater for vegetarians?

❹ 有沒有素食的選項？

⇨ Are there vegetarian options?

Part 01 圖解實用短句篇

Part 02 即時應答篇

MEMO

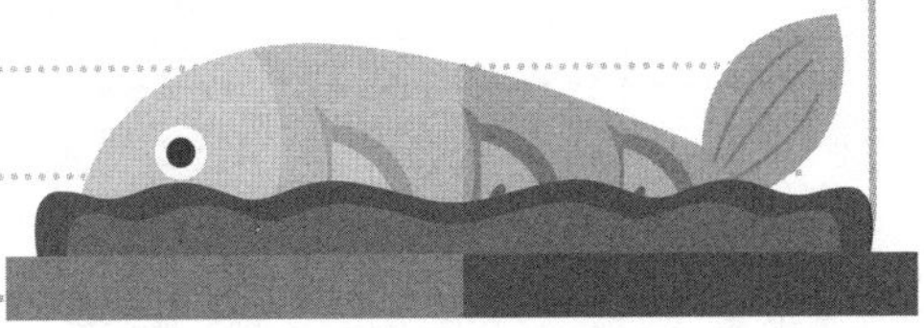

Q7 Do you have vegetarian food?
你們有素食的選項嗎？

Audrey Of course we do. We have a vegetarian menu and the selection is quite good. You can choose from pasta, pizza, vegetarian burger or wraps.

奧黛莉 我們當然有，而且種類還蠻多的，有義大利麵，披薩，素漢堡或是捲餅。

Sabrina Yes, we do, but the choices are quite limited. The only vegetarian food we have is pasta with assortment of mushrooms. If you take egg and milk, we can make it with cheese on top.

莎賓娜 有，我們有，可是選擇相當有限，我們的素食選項只有什錦菇義大利麵，如果你是奶蛋素的話，那我們可以在上面加上起司。

Dexter I am sorry, unfortunately we don't have a vegetarian menu. The closest thing we have would be French fries and jam on toast.

戴斯特 很抱歉我們沒有特製的素食選項，大概也只有薯條跟果醬吐司可以算是素食。

字彙表

selection	選項
limited	有限制的
assortment	綜合的
cheese on top	上面加起司

MEMO

超實用短句 1

❶ 你們有香烤豬排嗎？我不要炸的。

⇨ Do you have BBQ pork chop, I don't want the fried one.

❷ 豬排可以幫我用烤的嗎？ 不要用炸的。

⇨ Can I have my pork chop grilled, not fried please?

❸ 我想要乾麵，湯另外放。

⇨ Can I have my noodles dry please? And soup on the side.

❹ 我要燙青菜，不要炒的。

⇨ I prefer the vegetable steamed, not stir fried.

🔔 超實用短句 2

❶ 可以把皮烤脆一點嗎？

　⇨ Can you make the skin crispy?

❷ 我想要我的義大利麵煮軟一點。

　⇨ I prefer my pasta less Al dente.

❸ 我的魚排可以加多一點醬嗎？

　⇨ Can I have extra sauce on my fish please?

❹ 可以把雞肉切成小塊嗎？

　⇨ Can you chop the chicken into pieces please?

Part
01
圖解實用短句篇

Part
02
即時應答篇

MEMO

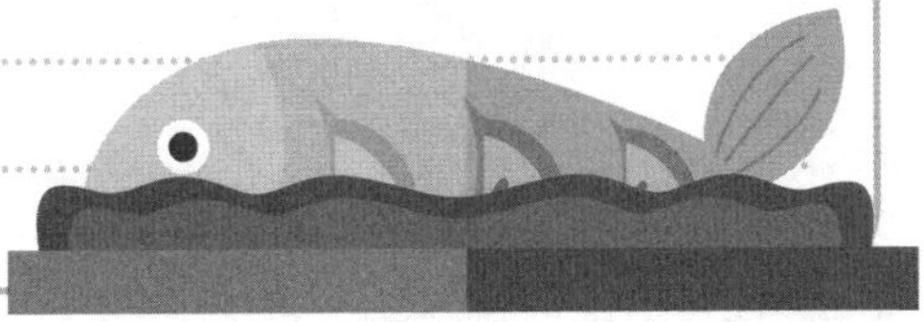

Q8 Do you prefer your fish grilled or steamed?

請問你的魚要烤的還是蒸的？

Audrey　Can I have my fish grilled with salt and pepper please? Does it come with lemon slices? I would love some lemon if possible.

奧黛莉　我想要椒鹽烤魚，請問有附檸檬嗎？如果沒有的話可以給我一點嗎？

Sabrina　I would prefer my fish steamed with extra garlic and spring onion. Can I have the sauce on top of the fish and vegetables please?

莎賓娜　我想要用蒸的，可以幫我加多一點蒜蓉還有蔥花嗎？麻煩你幫我把醬汁淋在於還有青菜上。

Dexter Do you do pan fry? I like the crispy skin. If you don't, then I will have my fish grilled. Can I have the sauce on the side please?

戴斯特 可以幫我用煎的嗎? 我喜歡脆口一點。如果不行的話,那就用烤的。麻煩你把醬汁放旁邊。

🍞 字彙表

al dente	偏硬的義大利麵口感
salt and pepper	椒鹽
garlic	蒜頭
spring onion	青蔥

MEMO

• UNIT9 •
飯店口味的濃淡

🔔 超實用短句 1

❶ 麻婆豆腐對我來說太辣了。
⇨ Ma-Po tofu is too spicy for me.

❷ 這個炒麵太鹹了。
⇨ This fried noodle is too salty.

❸ 這道菜有個苦味。
⇨ This dish tastes bitter to me.

❹ 沙拉醬不要太多。
⇨ I don't want too much salad dressing.

超實用短句 2

❶ 這湯不夠熱，可以熱一下嗎？

⇨ The soup is not hot enough, can you heat it up for me please?

❷ 我要不太辣的咖哩。

⇨ I prefer a mild curry.

❸ 這個炒飯味道不夠。

⇨ This fried rice is tasteless.

❹ 這個醬汁酸的無法入口。

⇨ This sauce is too sour to eat.

MEMO

Q9 How is your pasta?
這份義大利麵還合你的口味嗎？

Audrey Thanks, my pasta is good, just wondering whether you can bring me some cheese powder and freshly ground pepper please?

奧黛莉　謝謝你的詢問，這個義大利麵還不錯，可以麻煩你給我一點起司粉還有現磨糊椒嗎？

Sabrina I think the sauce is a bit bland, I think it needs extra salt and cheese. Can I have some parmesan cheese please?

莎賓娜　我的醬汁味道有點不夠，我覺得需要多加點鹽還有起司。可以給我一點帕曼森起司嗎？

Dexter The pasta is great! I like strong flavors and I really enjoy the chilly in the sauce. I will definitely come back again.

戴斯特 義大利麵很棒！我喜歡濃烈的味道，醬汁裡面的辣椒很夠味，我下次一定會再光臨的。

 字彙表

spicy	辣的
mild	微辣
tasteless	沒有味道
bland	平淡的

MEMO
....
....
....
....
....

飯店排餐的熟度

🔔 超實用短句 1

❶ 我喜歡全熟的牛排。

⇨ I prefer my steak well done

❷ 可以要 7 分熟的嗎？

⇨ Can I have my steak medium well please?

❸ 我要 5 分熟的就好。

⇨ I would like my steak medium please.

❹ 我要 3 分熟的。

⇨ Can I have my steak medium rare please?

🔔 超實用短句 2

❶ 這個煮太熟了。

⇨ It is a bit overcooked.

❷ 這個沒煮熟。

⇨ It is a bit under done.

❸ 這個煮得恰到好處。

⇨ It is just right.

❹ 這個燒焦了。

⇨ It is burnt.

MEMO

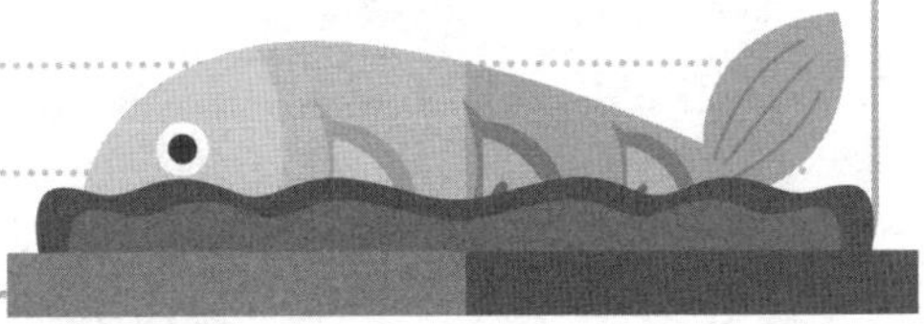

Q10 How would you like your steak?

你的牛排想要幾分熟呢？

Audrey　Can I have my steak well done please? I know it might be a bit tough, but I prefer it is fully cooked.

奧黛莉　我要全熟的，我知道可能會有點硬，可是我喜歡完全煮熟的。

Sabrina　I would like my steak medium rare, maybe more on the rare side. Please make sure the steak is not overcooked, otherwise it just becomes tough.

莎賓娜　我喜歡 3 分熟，可以生一點點無所謂，但是千萬不要太熟，因為肉就會硬掉。

Dexter Can I have my steak medium well please? I prefer a bit of pink in the middle. I think it is really juicy like that.

戴斯特 我喜歡 7 分熟，中間帶一點粉紅就最棒了。我覺得牛肉這樣最多汁。

 字彙表

medium well	**7 分熟**
medium rare	**3 分熟**
tough	硬的
juicy	多汁

MEMO

UNIT11
飯店好康折扣

🔔 超實用短句 1

❶ 壽星有折扣嗎？
⇨ Is there a discount for birthday girl?

❷ 小孩有折扣嗎？
⇨ Do you offer discount for kids?

❸ 學生有折扣嗎？
⇨ Do you do student discount?

❹ 當地人有折扣嗎？
⇨ Is there a discount for locals?

🔔 超實用短句 2

❶ 慶祝結婚紀念有折扣嗎？

⇨ Do you offer discounts for celebrating anniversary?

❷ 老人有折扣嗎？

⇨ Do you have senior discount?

❸ 付現金有折扣嗎？

⇨ Do you get a discount if you pay cash?

❹ 外帶會比較便宜嗎？

⇨ Is it cheaper if I order takeaway?

MEMO

Q11 Do you offer takeaway discount?
請問外帶有沒有折扣？

Audrey Yes, we do. You get a 10 % discount for takeaway. And if you order over 500 dollars, you get a free serving of spring rolls.

奧黛莉 有，當然有。外帶的話有一成的折扣，如果你點超過 500 元的餐點，我們還多送一份免費的春捲。

Sabrina Unfortunately, we don't offer a discount for takeaway, but we do offer a group discount if you order 5 main meals.

莎賓娜 不好意思我們沒有外帶的折扣，可是我們有團體折扣，點 5 份主餐就有折扣喔。

Dexter　Sorry we don't offer a discount for takeaway but we do give a 50 NT voucher for your next order if you order takeaway.

戴斯特　抱歉我們沒有外帶折扣，可是外帶的話會送 50 元的抵用券，可以下次用。

字彙表

one serve	一份
voucher	禮券、兌換券
coupon	優惠券
loyalty card	集點卡

MEMO

超實用短句 1

❶ 兩個人用餐有折扣嗎？

⇨ Do you offer any discount for two diners?

❷ 10 個人用餐可以不要算服務費嗎？

⇨ Can you waive the service charge if we order 10 meals?

❸ 點 3 份主餐會比較便宜嗎？

⇨ Do we get a discount if we order 3 meals?

❹ 點 5 杯奶茶會送一杯嗎？

⇨ Do we get a free milk tea if we order 5?

超實用短句 2

❶ 團體會有折扣嗎？

⇨ Do you offer group discount?

❷ 要訂多少才有批發價？

⇨ How much do we need to order to get the wholesale price?

❸ 買餐券等於有多折扣？

⇨ How much cheaper is the voucher compared with paying cash?

❹ 最少一次要買幾張餐券才有折扣？

⇨ How many meal vouchers do we need to buy to get the discount?

MEMO

Q12 Do you offer discounts for 5 people?
5 個人有折扣嗎？

Audrey Yes we do, we offer 10% discount for parties over 4 people. But each of the guests has to order a premier set menu.

奧黛莉 有的，只要有 4 個人就有九折優惠，但是每個人都要點一份精緻特餐。

Sabrina Unfortunately we don't offer any group discount, but we will waive the 10% service charge if you spend over 2500 NT.

莎賓娜 不好意思我們沒有團體折扣，可是如果結帳金額超過 2500 台幣的話，我們就免收服務費。

Dexter　I am sorry we don't have group discount, but we do have a value combo for two people. You save 300 NT if you order the combo.

戴斯特　抱歉我們沒有團體折扣，可是我們有兩人的超值套餐，點超值套餐的話可以省 300 元喔！

字彙表

service charge	服務費
wholesale price	批發價
compare with	跟某物比較
waive	免除、免收

MEMO

飯店折扣

超實用短句 1

❶ 平日用餐有折扣嗎？

⇨ Do you have any discount for weekdays?

❷ 周末可以用折價券嗎？

⇨ Can I use the coupon on the weekends?

❸ 兩點過後用餐有送飲料嗎？

⇨ Do you get a free drink for dining after 2 pm?

❹ 離峰時段用餐有折扣嗎？

⇨ Is there a discount if I come during off-peak hours?

🔔 超實用短句 2

❶ 寒假有折扣嗎？

⇨ Do you offer discount during school holiday in winter?

❷ 淡季的時候有折扣嗎？

⇨ Is there a discount during low season?

❸ 星期六的晚餐可以用信用卡優惠方案嗎？

⇨ Can I use the credit card deal for Saturday night dinner?

❹ 八點後入場有多少折扣嗎？

⇨ How much discount do you offer for coming after 8 pm?

MEMO

Q13 Can I use the coupon on the weekends?

週末可以用折價券嗎？

Audrey I am sorry, the coupon is only good for the weekdays. We don't accept the coupon on the weekends. The coupon is only valid for weekday lunch.

奧黛莉 很抱歉折價券只能平日使用，我們假日不收。而且平日的話也僅限午餐使用。

Sabrina Yes you can, but there is a condition, you can only use one coupon for food orders, not for drink orders.

莎賓娜 當然可以，可是有個限制，折價券只能折抵餐點，不能折抵飲料。

Dexter　Sure, you can. But the coupon is limited to one coupon per table per main meal. The others will be charged at full price.

戴斯特　當然可以，可是折價券一桌只能折一份主餐，其他的會以原價計算。

字彙表

accept	接受
valid for	某時段可以用
conditions	條件、限制
full price	原價、定價

超實用短句 1

❶ 可以帶外食嗎？

⇨ Can I bring outside food?

❷ 可不可以自己帶紅酒？

⇨ Can I bring my own wine?

❸ 可以請你們準備蛋糕嗎？

⇨ Can you organize the cake for me?

❹ 我的婚宴可以雇用餐廳的主持人嗎？

⇨ Can I hire your restaurant MC to host my wedding party?

🔔 超實用短句 2

❶ 可以請服務生幫我把裝飾品佈置一下嗎？

⇨ Can I have the waiters to help me hang the decorations?

❷ 可以把這兩桌併起來嗎？

⇨ Can I move these two tables together?

❸ 可以提供包廂嗎？

⇨ Can we use the private rooms?

❹ 最晚幾點要離場？

⇨ When is the latest we need to leave?

MEMO

Q14 Do you do BYO (Bring your own) drinks?

可以自己帶飲料嗎?

Audrey   Yes, we do, but only for wine, because we sell soft drinks and beer. For each bottle of wine we charge 50 NT for corkage.

⊕

奧黛莉   可以的,但是只能帶紅酒類,因為我們本身有賣汽水跟啤酒。要提醒您每一罐酒會收 50 元的開瓶費。

Sabrina   Unfortunately, we don't do BYO drinks. All the drinks have to be purchased from the restaurant. We do provide free water.

⊕

莎賓娜   不好意思客人不能自己帶飲料。所有的飲料都需要跟餐廳選購,但是我們有免費提供水。

Dexter Sure you can, you can bring your own beer or wine, but we do have a good selection of wine in the restaurant if you prefer to order here.

戴斯特 當然可以,你可以自己帶啤酒或紅酒,但是如果你不想帶的話,我們餐廳也有很有種類可供選擇。

 **字彙表**

MC (Master of ceremonies)	主持人
BYO (Bring your own)	自己帶
purchase	購買
provide	提供

MEMO

超實用短句 1

❶ 有外送的服務嗎？

⇨ Do you do delivery?

❷ 可以外送到金沙酒店嗎？

⇨ Can you deliver to Golden Sand hotel?

❸ 外送的最低金額是多少？

⇨ What's the minimum order for delivery?

❹ 外送大概要等多久？

⇨ Roughly how long do we need to wait for?

超實用短句 2

❶ 如果可以的話，麻煩你剩下的要外帶。

⇨ I would like to take away the leftover if I can.

❷ 我要外帶一份烤雞。

⇨ Can I order a serve a BBQ chicken to take away please?

❸ 烤雞需要預定還是現場就有？

⇨ Do I need to pre order a BBQ chicken or it is available anytime?

❹ 義大利麵可以外帶嗎？

⇨ Do you do take away pasta?

MEMO

Q15 Do you do delivery?

你們有外送嗎？

Audrey Unfortunately we don't have enough manpower to do delivery. You are more than welcome to order dine in or takeaway.

奧黛莉 不好意思我們人手不夠，無法外送。但是你可以點內用或外帶喔!

Sabrina Yes, we do, there is no minimum order but for each order we charge 50NT for delivery. If you order over 1000 NT, then the delivery is free.

莎賓娜 我們可以，外送的話是沒有最低金額，可是每筆外送我們酌收 50 元的外送費。如果點餐金額超過 1000 元的話，那外送就免收費。

Dexter　Of course, we do. The minimum order for delivery is NT 500, and we only deliver to areas that are within 5 kilometers away.

戴斯特　當然有，外送最少要點 500 元以上，我們只有送到 5 公里之內的地方喔。

🍔 字彙表

minimum	最少
roughly	大概
manpower	人力、人手
dine in	內用

MEMO

飯店廁所

🍱 超實用短句 1

❶ 廁所好髒喔。
⇨ The toilet is filthy.

❷ 廁所裡有小蟲。
⇨ There is a bug in the toilet.

❸ 這味道好臭。我在外面就可以聞廁所的臭味了。
⇨ It is so stinky; I can smell it from the outside.

❹ 廁所沒有衛生紙了,麻煩你們補充一下。
⇨ There is no toilet paper in the toilet, can you refill it please?

超實用短句 2

❶ 廁所的馬桶塞住了。我沒辦法沖。

⇨ The toilet is blocked. I can't flush it.

❷ 廁所的地板很濕滑,超危險的。

⇨ The toilet floor is very slippery, it is very dangerous.

❸ 可以請人去清一下廁所嗎?

⇨ Can you send someone to go and clean the toilet please?

❹ 有人吐在地板上。真的很噁心。

⇨ Someone puked on the floor. It is disgusting.

Part 01 圖解實用短句篇

Part 02 即時應答篇

MEMO

Q16 Can you send someone to go and clean the toilet please?

可以麻煩您派人去清一下廁所嗎？

Audrey Of course, we will send someone right away, may I ask what is wrong with the toilet? If it is a blockage, I will need to call the plumber.

奧黛莉　當然，我們會馬上派人去看看，請問是哪裡有問題，如果是塞住的話，那我要請水電工來。

Sabrina I am very sorry, we are very busy at the moment. I will send someone to clean the toilet as soon as possible.

莎賓娜　很抱歉我們目前很忙，我會盡快派人去整理廁所。

Dexter　Sure, thanks for letting us know. The toilet was cleaned not long ago. I will send someone to go and have a look again.

戴斯特　沒問題，謝謝你跟我們反應，廁所剛剛才整理過，我會再派個人過去看看。

字彙表

blocked	塞住、卡住
flush	沖水
slippery	很滑
puke	嘔吐

MEMO

飯店餐點裡有異物

🔔 超實用短句 1

❶ 我的麵裡有頭髮。

⇨ There is a hair in my noodles.

❷ 這裡面好像有隻蒼蠅，太噁心了。

⇨ There is fly in it. It is so disgusting.

❸ 這明明就是蟑螂腳。

⇨ This is definitely a cockroach leg.

❹ 這炒蛋裡面有蛋殼，我差點吞下去。

⇨ There is egg shell in this scramble egg. I almost swallowed it.

🔔 超實用短句 2

❶ 這醬汁裡面怎麼會有小石頭。

⇨ How come there is a small rock in the sauce?

❷ 魚排的刺沒有挑乾淨。魚刺卡在我的喉嚨。

⇨ There are bones in this fish fillet. It stuck in my throat.

❸ 這杯飲料裡面有螞蟻。

⇨ There is an ant in my drink.

❹ 有隻小蟲飛進去我的湯裡。

⇨ There is a bug landed in my soup.

MEMO

Q17 There is a bug in my food, I want my money back.

我的餐點裡面有隻小蟲，我要退錢！

Audrey I am very sorry, we apologize for the inconvenience caused. I will get the kitchen to make a new one for you, but we usually have a no refund policy.

奧黛莉 我真的很抱歉，造成您的不便了！我會請廚房再做一份新的給您，我們通常是不退款的。

Sabrina Oh, my Goodness. My apology, I will let the kitchen know. We don't do cash refunds, Can I offer you a gift voucher for your next visit?

莎賓娜 天啊，我真的很抱歉，我會馬上跟廚房反應。我們沒辦法退錢。我可以給以餐廳的禮券嗎?您下回可以用。

Dexter I am so sorry, can I get the kitchen to make you a new one? We don't do cash refunds, but your meal will be free of charge.

戴斯特 我真的很抱歉,我馬上請廚房做一份新的給您。我們沒辦法退錢,可是您今天的餐點是免費的。

字彙表

disgusting	噁心、令人作嘔
swallow	吞下
stuck	卡住
free of charge	免費

MEMO

飯店食物沒煮熟

超實用短句 1

❶ 我的魚裡面還是生的，請幫我重做一份。

⇨ My fish is raw inside, please take it back and make a new one.

❷ 我的烤雞只有外面是熟的。

⇨ The BBQ chicken is only cooked on the outside.

❸ 這個烤肉串沒有烤熟。

⇨ This kebab is not cooked through.

❹ 這個水煮蛋的蛋黃太生了。

⇨ The yolk of this boil egg is too runny.

🔔 超實用短句 2

❶ 我的羊排裡面還是冰的，我沒辦法吃，請退回去。

⇨ My lamb chop is frozen inside. I can't eat it, please take it back.

❷ 這個牛排太生了，可以幫我再煎熟一點嗎？

⇨ The steak is too rare for me, can you cook it a bit longer please?

❸ 這個義大利麵太硬了。

⇨ This pasta is too al dente.

❹ 這個餅乾中間沒烤熟。

⇨ The center of the cookie is too gooey.

MEMO

Q18 The waiter came and got me, is there a problem with your meal?

服務生説您要見我，請問餐點有問題嗎？

Audrey I ordered my steak medium well, but this is way too rare for me. Can you get the kitchen to make me a new one please?

奧黛莉　我點的牛排是七分熟，可是這個實在太生了，可以請廚房重做一份嗎？

Sabrina This omelet is too runny inside, I can't eat it, can you bring it back and make sure they fully cook the eggs please?

莎賓娜　我烘蛋裡面煮的不夠熟，我沒但法吃這麼生的，可以拿會去重做一份嗎？蛋要全熟喔！

Dexter The roast vegetable is not cooked long enough. The potatoes and the carrots are still crunchy in the center. I can't eat it.

戴斯特 這個焗烤蔬菜沒烤熟，馬鈴薯根紅蘿蔔的中心都還是硬的，這怎麼吃啊！

字彙表

raw	生的
cooked through	煮熟了
runny	流質的、像水狀沒有熟
gooey	黏稠的、軟軟的沒有熟

• UNIT19 •
飯店付款問題

🔔 超實用短句 1

❶ 可以只匯訂金就好嗎？
 ⇨ Can we pay just the deposit?

❷ 現在一定要付清全額嗎？
 ⇨ Do I have to pay in full now?

❸ 可以用信用卡付款嗎？
 ⇨ Do you accept credit card?

❹ 可以退房時再付款嗎？
 ⇨ Can I pay on check out?

超實用短句 2

❶ 臨時取消要扣多少錢？

⇨ How much is your cancellation charge?

❷ 手續費要扣多少？

⇨ How much is the fees?

❸ 如果要續住房價怎麼算？

⇨ How much do you charge if we stay extra nights?

❹ 請問收不收旅行支票？

⇨ Do you accept travelers cheques?

MEMO

Q19 How much do you charge for cancellation?

取消的話你們怎麼收費？

Audrey If you cancel 30 days in advance, then you can have a full refund, we charge 50% after that, and if you cancel on the same day, then we charge 100%.

奧黛莉 如果你 30 天前取消的話，我們全額退費。可是 30 天以內的話我們就會收 5 成的費用，如果你當天才取消的話，我們必須收取全額的費用。

Sabrina The credit card detail you provided is only to guarantee your booking. There is no cancellation, but if you do not show up for your booking, we would charge for one day.

莎賓娜 您提供的信用卡資料只是幫您保留房間，取消的話沒有費用，但是如果你們沒有取消而且沒有入住的話，那我們會收一個晚上的錢。

Dexter　This is a non-refundable booking; therefore, if you decided to cancel the booking, you will still get charged the full amount. Please think again before you book.

戴斯特　這是無法取消的專案，如果你訂了之後要取消的話，那我們也無法退款。訂房錢請您要想清楚。

字彙表

pay in full	全額付清
cancellation	取消
travelers cheques	旅行支票
in advance	之前、預先

MEMO

· UNIT20 ·
飯店服務

超實用短句 1

❶ 有沒有含早餐？

⇨ Is breakfast included?

❷ 有沒有雙人房？

⇨ Is double room available?

❸ 有沒有家庭房？

⇨ Do you have family room?

❹ 有沒有含晚餐？

⇨ Is dinner provided?

 **超實用短句 2**

❶ 有沒有含下午茶？
⇨ Is afternoon tea included?

❷ 有沒有含機場接送？
⇨ Do you have free airport shuttle?

❸ 有沒有含網路？
⇨ Do you have free internet connection?

❹ 是不是免費停車？
⇨ Do you charge for parking?

MEMO

Q20 Is breakfast included in our booking?

我們訂的房型有含早餐嗎？

Audrey　Let me check for you. Yes, breakfast is included in your booking. Breakfast is available between 6-10 am at our pool side restaurant.

奧黛莉　讓我幫你查一下。有的你的房型有含早餐，早餐供應的時間是 6-10 點，在池畔餐廳。

Sabrina　No, unfortunately this is a room only booking, if you would like to add breakfast, it will be USD 15 each for adults and half price for kids under 12.

莎賓娜　不好意思你的房型並沒有含早餐，如果你要加購早餐的話，大人每人 15 美金，12 歲以下的小孩半價。

Dexter Yes, there are two breakfast included for each room. Since there are three of you, would you like to add one more breakfast?

戴斯特 有的你的房型有含兩客早餐，既然你們有三個人，需要加一份早餐嗎？

 **字彙表**

room only	純住房、不含早餐
breakfast included	含早餐
continental breakfast	歐陸式早餐（較簡單，通常只有咖啡，麵包麥片類）
full breakfast	全早餐（通常是自助式早餐，有熱食的）

MEMO

飯店設施

🔔 超實用短句 1

❶ 請問游泳池早上幾點開放？

⇨ What time does the pool open in the morning?

❷ 泳池是溫水的嗎？

⇨ Is the pool heated?

❸ 需要戴泳帽嗎？

⇨ Do I need to wear a swimming cap?

❹ 游泳池有提供浴巾嗎？

⇨ Is the towel provided at the pool?

超實用短句 2

❶ 請問有兒童遊戲室嗎？

⇨ Do you have a kids play room?

❷ 健身房開到幾點？

⇨ What time does the gym close?

❸ 商務中心怎們收費？

⇨ How do you charge for using the business center?

❹ 退房後可以寄放行李嗎？

⇨ Can you store our bags for me after we check out?

MEMO

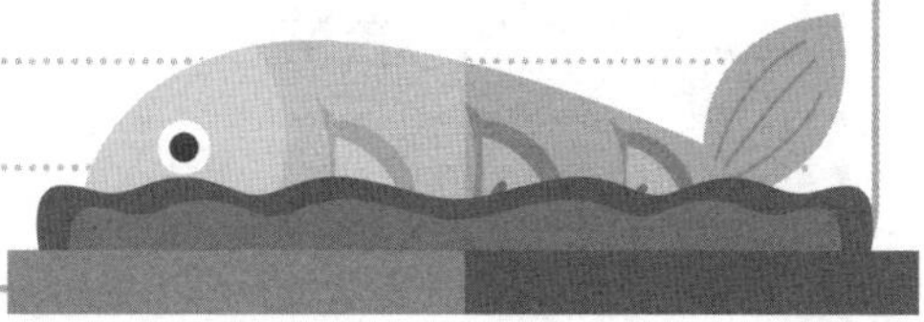

Q21 How do you charge for using the business center?

請問使用商務中心你們怎麼收費？

Audrey If you stay in a business suite, you get to use the business center for free. If you are in a hotel, we charge by the hour, it is NTD 250 per hour.

奧黛莉 如果您是商務房的房客，那使用商務中心是免費的。如果你是一般房客，那每個小時是台幣 250 元。

Sabrina Unfortunately we don't have a business center here, but we have a coin operated computer with internet connection at level 2. It is NTD 50 for half an hour.

莎賓娜 不好意思我們沒有商務中心，可是我們二樓有投幣式的電腦，可以上網，半個小時是 50 台幣。

Dexter   We charge by the slot of 3 hours. You have to book in advance to ensure it is available. Each time slot is NTD 800.

戴斯特　我們每次以三小時計費，客人需要提早預約，每次的費用是台幣 800 元。

 **字彙表**

coin operated	投幣式的
internet connection	網路連線
time slot	時段
ensure	確認

MEMO

超實用短句 1

❶ 請問房間冷氣怎麼調小一點？

⇨ Can you tell me how do I turn the air condition down please?

❷ 我的暖氣沒有功用。

⇨ The heater in my room is not working.

❸ 我的保險箱打不開，系統好像壞掉了？

⇨ I can't open my safe. I think the system is not working properly.

❹ 請問電話如何打外線？

⇨ How do I call out?

超實用短句 2

❶ 可以告訴我電話怎麼打隔壁房嗎？

⇨ Can you tell me how to call next door please?

❷ 請問燈的總開關在哪裡？

⇨ Where is the master switch for the lights?

❸ 請問窗戶怎麼開？

⇨ How do I open the window?

❹ 電視的遙控器沒電了。

⇨ The TV remote is out of battery.

MEMO

Q22 Can you tell me how to adjust the air conditioner please?

請問房間的冷氣該怎麼使用？

Audrey　You will see a dial on the wall, and if you want to turn it up, just turn it to the left, and if you want to turn it off, just turn it all the way to the end.

奧黛莉　你在牆上會看到一個控制鈕，如果以要強一點，就向左轉，要弱一點，就像右轉。如果要關掉就向右轉到底。

Sabrina　The air condition we got is the reverse cycle. Make sure you have the setting set to "Cool" instead of "Heat" then all you have to do is to adjust the temperature to your liking.

莎賓娜　我們的空調是冷熱兩用機，你要確認一下設定選擇冷氣不是熱風，然後再選擇溫度即可。

Dexter　There are three settings for the air conditioner, which are " Fan," "Low," and "High" You can change it with the remote control.

戴斯特　我們的空調只有三段設定，送風、弱跟強。你可以用遙控器選擇。

字彙表

setting	控制、設定
reverse cycle	冷熱兩用機
temperature	溫度
remote control	遙控器

飯店客房服務

🔔 超實用短句 1

❶ 麻煩你幫我多送一床棉被。

⇨ Can you bring me extra set of blanket please?

❷ 麻煩你幫我加床。

⇨ We need a rollout bed in our room please.

❸ 我需要多一個枕頭。

⇨ I would like to have an extra pillow.

❹ 請問這麼晚了還可以叫客房服務嗎？

⇨ Can we order room service this time of the day?

超實用短句 2

❶ 我的房間今天不需要整理。

⇨ My room does not need to be made up today.

❷ 可以再給我幾個茶包嗎？

⇨ Can I have extra tea bags please?

❸ 房間廁所的衛生紙沒有了。

⇨ Can you top up the toilet papers please?

❹ 明天早上可以幫我送一份報紙嗎？

⇨ Can you delivery a newspaper to my room
tomorrow morning please?

MEMO

Q23 Can we order room service at this time of day?

請問這麼晚了還可以叫客房服務嗎？

Audrey Sure you can, we are still taking room service orders, there is a room service menu right by the phone. I will transfer you to the kitchen, please hold.

奧黛莉 當然可以，我們的客房服務還有開放，在電話的旁有一份菜單，我幫你轉接給廚房。

Sabrina Unfortunately the kitchen is closed. If you would like to order something to eat, there are premade sandwiches from the café. I can get them delivered to you.

莎賓娜 不好意思廚房已經關了，如果您想要點吃的東西的話，我們有咖啡廳現成的三明治，我可以幫您安排送上去。

Dexter Unfortunately the kitchen is closed. There are a few menus in the drawer from nearby restaurants; they are still open and they will deliver to the hotel.

戴斯特 不好意思廚房已經關了，在抽屜裡有幾份附近餐廳的菜單，他們還開著，也會幫您送到飯店。

字彙表

please hold	電話轉接中
premade	現成的、預先做好的
nearby	附近
tips	小費

MEMO

超實用短句 1

❶ 請問時代廣場怎麼去？

⇨ Can you tell me how to get to Time square please?

❷ 你會建議我們怎麼去？

⇨ What would you suggest us to do?

❸ 坐火車比較方便還是搭巴士？

⇨ What's the best way? Train or bus?

❹ 你們有免費的市區地圖嗎？

⇨ Do you have a free city map?

♨ 超實用短句 2

❶ 搭巴士去大概多少錢？

⇨ How much does the bus cost?

❷ 這裡有租車公司嗎？

⇨ Is there a car rental company here?

❸ 租車有含 GPS 嗎？

⇨ Is the GPS included?

❹ 搭地鐵去大概要多久？

⇨ How long does it take if we take subway?

MEMO

Q24 What would you suggest us to do?
你會建議我們怎麼去？

Audrey　I would suggest you take the shuttle bus to the bus terminal. Then you can get on the number 213 bus to Universal Studios. It will drop you off right at the entrance.

奧黛莉　我會建議你搭接駁車到巴士總站，然後你可以搭 213 號巴士去環球影城，它會直接帶你到門口。

Sabrina　I think the best way is to go by train, for the two of you it will probably cost less than driving across and you will get there quicker too.

莎賓娜　我覺得最好的方式是搭火車去，你們兩個人的話可能比開車的油錢便宜，而且也比較快。

Dexter I will suggest you take the subway to the pier and then take the ferry across to the south side. The zoo is only 10 minutes' walk from the ferry terminal.

戴斯特 我會建議你搭地鐵到碼頭,然後從碼頭搭渡輪到南邊,動物園離碼頭(渡輪站)大概走路 10 分鐘就到了。

 **字彙表**

entrance	門口、入口
cost less than	比（某物）便宜
bus terminal	巴士站
ferry terminal	渡輪站

🔔 超實用短句 1

❶ 你們有代訂旅遊的服務嗎？

⇨ Do you have a tour booking desk?

❷ 哪個行程是你們最推的？

⇨ What is the most popular tour here?

❸ 有一日遊嗎？

⇨ Do you have day tour?

❹ 我想參加遊船的行程。

⇨ I would like to do the river cruise.

超實用短句 2

1 第二個人有折扣嗎？

⇨ Is there a discount for more than one person?

2 行程有含飯店接送嗎？

⇨ Do they pick up and drop off from the hotel?

3 行程的費用有含入場門票嗎？

⇨ Is the entry fee included as part of the cost?

4 迪士尼幾點關門？

⇨ What time does Disney open until?

MEMO

Q25 What is the most popular tour here?
哪個行程是你們最推的？

Audrey　The most popular tour here is the evening mangrove cruise. You get to see the monkeys and the fireflies. A light dinner is included, too.

奧黛莉　我們最受歡迎的行程是夜間紅樹林遊船，你可以看到猴子還有螢火蟲，也有供應簡單的晚餐。

Sabrina　What do you prefer to do? Our river kayaking is very popular if you are looking for something active, if you prefer sightseeing tours, then I will suggest you do the botanical garden tour.

莎賓娜　你們喜歡做怎麼樣的活動？如果你們喜歡動態的，那野溪獨木舟我很推薦，如果你要靜態的觀光行程，那我建議你可以參加植物園之旅。

Dexter　Are you looking for day tours or overnight trips? Our one day volcano visit if very popular and it can be combined into a two day volcano and cultural village visit.

戴斯特　你們要當天來回的還是要過夜的？我們的火山之旅很受歡迎，可以當天來回，或是跟文化村的行程併成兩天一夜。

字彙表

firefly	螢火蟲
kayaking	划獨木舟
sightseeing	觀光
botanical garden	植物園

MEMO

飯店接駁車

🔔 超實用短句 1

❶ 接駁車一天有幾班?

⇨ How many runs does the shuttle bus do each day?

❷ 下一班車幾點來?

⇨ What time is the next bus?

❸ 請問回程的時候在哪裡上車?

⇨ Where do we wait for the bus on our way back?

❹ 最後一班車是幾點?

⇨ What time is the last shuttle?

超實用短句 2

❶ 接駁車需要預訂嗎？

⇨ Do we need to book the shuttle bus?

❷ 接駁車是免費嗎？

⇨ Is the shuttle bus free?

❸ 接駁車有到環球影城嗎？

⇨ Does the shuttle bus drop you off at Universal studio?

❹ 接駁車總共停幾個站？

⇨ How many stops does the bus go?

MEMO

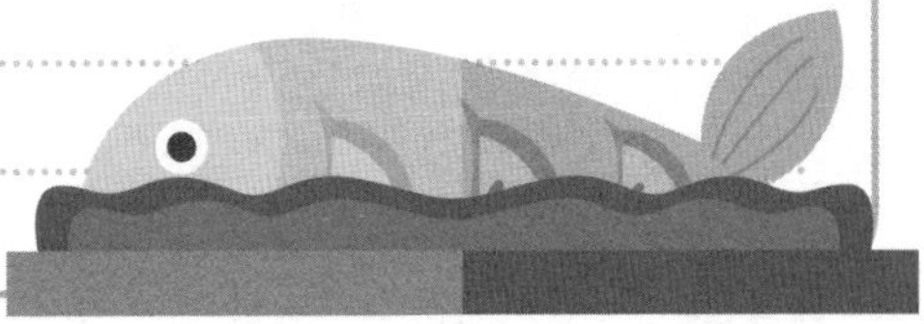

Q26 Where does the shuttle bus go?

接駁車總共停幾個站?

Audrey The shuttle bus takes you to most of the major tourist attractions, such as the Opera house, circular quay, and the rocks, then it takes you back to Darling harbor.

奧黛莉 接駁車會帶你待主要的觀光景點,例如歌劇院、環形碼頭、岩石區然後帶你回達令港。

Sabrina The bus goes between the hotel and the airport, it goes via downtown, and you can choose to get off at Raffles shopping center or the post office.

莎賓娜 接駁車的路線是飯店到機場,中途會經過市區,你可以在萊佛士購物中心下車或是郵局。

Dexter The shuttle bus takes you to the beach and back. There are only 12 seats on the bus, but we don't take any bookings. It is first come first serve.

戴斯特 接駁車的路線是飯店到海邊,但是每台車只有 12 個位子,你不需要預定,直接現場排隊。

字彙表

shuttle bus	接駁車
downtown	市中心
via	經過、透過
first come first serve	先到先得、現場排隊

MEMO

飯店訂房折扣

🔔 超實用短句 1

❶ 請問房客用餐有折扣嗎？

⇨ Do you offer a dinning discount for hotel guests?

❷ 房客可以免費使用健身房嗎？

⇨ Is the gym free for the hotel guests?

❸ 我聽說房客可以免費使用商務中心 1 小時。

⇨ I was told the hotel guests can use the business center for free for one hour.

❹ 房客可以免費停車嗎？

⇨ Is the parking free for hotel guests?

🔔 超實用短句 2

❶ 每間客房有 2 張免費的迎賓飲料券。

⇨ You get two free drink vouchers each room.

❷ 房客用餐免收服務費。

⇨ Service charge is waived for hotel guests at the restaurants.

❸ 餐費可以掛房帳嗎？

⇨ Can we charge the restaurant bill to the room?

❹ 續住平日打 6 折。

⇨ You get 40% off if you staying extra nights during weekdays.

MEMO

Q27 **Do you offer a dinning discount for hotel guests?**

請問房客用餐有折扣嗎？

Audrey Yes, we do, if you dine at our roof top restaurant, the service charge will be waived for hotel guests. You can save 10% of the total bill.

奧黛莉 有的，如果房客在我們的屋頂餐廳用餐的話，免收服務費，您可以省 1 成的費用。

Sabrina Unfortunately, we don't offer any cash discount for hotel guests, but you get a free welcome drink from the lobby piano bar.

莎賓娜 不好意思我們沒有提供現金折扣，可是如果您到大廳鋼琴酒吧的話，會有一杯免費的迎賓飲料。

Dexter　Of course, we do, all hotel guests are entitled to a 10% discount when you spend more than NTD 5000 per table in our Steakhouse.

戴斯特　我們當然有，在我們牛排館每桌用餐超過 5000 千元的話，就可以享有九折。

🍔 字彙表

roof top	頂樓
welcome drink	迎賓飲料
lobby	飯店大廳
be entitled to	享有

MEMO

超實用短句 1

❶ 可以請給我間單人房嗎？

⇨ Can I have a single room please?

❷ 我要兩小床的房型。

⇨ I would like a twin room.

❸ 你們的家庭房是有上下舖的那種嗎？

⇨ Is there a bunk bed in your family room?

❹ 家庭房可以住幾個人？

⇨ How many people can you accommodate in your family room?

 **超實用短句 2**

❶ 有沒有小木屋？

⇨ Do you have cabins?

❷ 可以給我們相通的房間嗎？

⇨ Can you give us adjoining rooms please?

❸ 一間雙人房最多可以加幾個人？

⇨ What is the maximum guests allowed in a double room?

❹ 有三人房嗎？

⇨ Do you have triple room?

MEMO

Q28 Can you give us adjoining rooms please?

可以給我們相通的房間嗎？

Audrey   Sure, the only adjoining rooms we have is one room with one double bed and other has twin beds. Would this be ok?

奧黛莉   當然，可是我們相通的房間其中一間是一大床，另一間是兩小床，可以嗎？

Sabrina   Unfortunately, we don't have any adjoining rooms available. The best I can do is to have both of your room next to each other. Is this ok?

莎賓娜   不好意思我們沒有相通的房間，我可以幫你找兩間相連的隔壁房好嗎？

Dexter　Our adjoining rooms are at the far end of the west wing and we are renovating the rooms nearby. It will be quite noisy, would it be ok?

戴斯特　我們相連的房間在西翼樓最遠的那端，而且附近的房間都在整修，會有點吵，這樣可以接受嗎？

字彙表

adjoining room	相通的房間
twin beds	兩小床
renovation	整修
far end	最遠的那一端

MEMO

🔔 超實用短句 1

❶ 可以幫我請醫生來嗎？

⇨ Can you send a doctor here please?

❷ 趕快叫救護車！

⇨ Please call the ambulance!

❸ 麻煩你外送到 502 房。

⇨ Please delivery to Room 502.

❹ 請問有沒有 OK 蹦，我割到手。

⇨ Can I have a plaster please? I accidently cut my
finger.

超實用短句 2

❶ 飯店裡有日用品販賣部嗎？

⇨ Do you have a kiosk counter here?

❷ 可以在櫃檯換錢嗎？

⇨ Do you do currency exchange at the front desk?

❸ 可以幫我把行李送到房間去嗎？

⇨ Can you delivery my luggage to my room please.

❹ 可以幫我叫計程車嗎？

⇨ Can you order me a taxi please?

MEMO

Q29 Do you do currency exchange at the front desk?
可以在櫃檯換錢嗎？

Audrey Of course, we do but we charge a 1% fee. Make sure you bring your passport with you and we take all major currencies.

奧黛莉 當然可以，可是我們收百分之 1 的手續費，記得要帶您的護照，主要貨幣我們都收。

Sabrina Unfortunately, we don't have a currency exchange at our front desk. There is a currency exchange counter nearby. Just turn left at the intersection and it is on your right hand side.

莎賓娜 不好意思我們櫃台不能換外幣，這附近有外幣匯兌的地方，走到路口左轉，就在你的右手邊。

Dexter Yes, we do currency exchange but we only take USD, AUD, EUR and Singaporean dollars. Unfortunately, we don't take Taiwanese dollars; you can try at the bank.

戴斯特 可以，可是我們只收美金、澳幣、歐元還有新加坡幣。不好意思我們不收台幣，你可以去銀行試試看。

🍞 字彙表

kiosk	零售部、販賣部
luggage	行李
currency exchange	外幣兌換
intersection	路口

MEMO

🔔 **超實用短句 1**

❶ 房間有 WIFI 嗎？

⇨ Do you have WIFI in the lobby?

❷ 大廳的 WIFI 密碼是多少？

⇨ What is the password for lobby WIFI?

❸ WIFI 需要密碼嗎？

⇨ Do I need passwords to connect to WIFI?

❹ WIFI 是免費的嗎？

⇨ Is the WIFI free of charge?

🔔 超實用短句 2

❶ 我房間的 WIFI 連不上。

⇨ I can't connect to the WIFI in my room.

❷ WIFI 的收訊不好，可以連隔壁房間的嗎？

⇨ The WIFI connection is very bad in my room, can I used the connection from next door?

❸ 這個 WIFI 未免也太慢了吧？

⇨ This WIFI is way too slow.

❹ WIFI 的費用是怎麼算的？

⇨ How do you charge for WIFI?

MEMO

Q30 The WIFI keeps dropping out, do you have other WIFI account?

這個 WIFI 一直斷線，你們有沒有其他的 WIFI 帳號？

Audrey Our apology, the WIFI is a bit unstable sometimes. We have lots of guests staying today, so the reception will be affected. I am very sorry we don't have another account.

🔈

奧黛莉 很抱歉，這個 WIFI 有時候很不穩定，我們今天有很多客人，所以收訊號不穩。很抱歉我們沒有別的帳號。

Sabrina Yes, we do. Try to link with lobby01, I think that one works better. You will need to enter the password. The password is hotel1234.

🔈

莎賓娜 有的，你試試看 lobby01 這個帳號，會比較穩定。可以你需要密碼，密碼是 hotel1234。

Dexter　I would suggest to try the WIFI in the room. There is one account for each room. I think that one will work much better.

🔄

戴斯特　我建議你試試看房間的 WIFI，每個房間有自己專屬的，會好很多。

🍴 字彙表

signal	訊號
drop out	斷線
unstable	不穩定的
reception	收訊

MEMO

UNIT31
飯店機場接送

超實用短句 1

❶ 請問機場接送多少錢？
⇨ How much do you charge for airport pick up?

❷ 接送是算人數還是算趟？
⇨ Do you charge by per person or by per trip?

❸ 機場接送巴士的站牌在哪裡？
⇨ Where can I find the bus stop for the airport shuttle?

❹ 需要先買車票嗎？還是上車再付？
⇨ Do I need to get tickets first? Or I can pay while on the bus?

超實用短句 2

❶ 坐計程車到機場大概多少錢？

⇨ How much does the taxi cost to go to the airport?

❷ 我想要確認我預訂了機場接送。

⇨ I would like to reconfirm my booking for airport shuttle.

❸ 我的班機會延誤 2 小時，我要修改接機的時間。

⇨ I need to amend the pickup time; my flight is delayed by two hours.

❹ 請問機場接送要多久以前預訂？

⇨ When do I have to book the airport shuttle?

MEMO

Q31 How much do you charge for airport pick up?

請問機場接送多少錢？

Audrey　How many of you? If there is only one of you, then I will suggest you take the airport shuttle, we charge USD 100 for pick up, but it is for up to 4 people.

奧黛莉　你們有幾個人？如果只有你一個的話，我建議你搭機場接駁車，我們的接送一趟是 100 美金，可以坐 4 個人。

Sabrina　We charge USD 30 per person for the airport shuttle. If you book two weeks in advance, we offer a 10% discount. Should I take your booking now?

莎賓娜　機場接駁車是一個人 30 美金，如果你兩星期前訂的話，那有 1 成的折扣。要幫您訂什麼時候呢？

Dexter Unfortunately we don't run our own airport pick up, you can take the airport shuttle from terminal two, and let the driver know where you going and he will drop you off at our hotel.

戴斯特 不好意思我們沒有自己的機場接送,你可以在二航廈外搭機場接駁車,跟司機說要到這裡,他就會送你到飯店門口了。

字彙表

delayed	延誤了
up to 4 people	最多 **4** 人
terminal two	第二航廈
drop off	放下、帶你到某處

MEMO

🔔 超實用短句 1

❶ 隔壁吵得我受不了，請幫我換房間。

⇨ Can you transfer me to a different room please? I can't stand noise from next door.

❷ 水壺壞掉請幫我換一個。

⇨ Can you bring me a new kettle please? This one is not working.

❸ 這杯子沒洗乾淨，請拿一個新的來。

⇨ The glass is filthy, please bring the new one for me.

❹ 這床單上有污漬，請房務部幫我換一條。

⇨ There is a stain on the sheets; can you get the housekeeper to replace it please?

🔔 **超實用短句 2**

❶ 我的房卡沒辦法感應，可以幫我檢查一下嗎？
⇨ My key card does not work, can you check it for me please?

❷ 這條浴巾上有破洞，請換一條。
⇨ There is a hole on the bath towel, can you replace it for me please?

❸ 這個電話故障了，麻煩你幫我換一個。
⇨ The phone is not working; I would like to have a new one.

❹ 這個拖鞋的尺寸太小，麻煩你換大一號。
⇨ The slipper is too small; can you give me a bigger size?

Q32 Can you transfer me to a different room please? I can't stand the noise from next door.

隔壁吵得我受不了,請幫我換房間。

Audrey I am very sorry. I will call them straight away and ask they to keep the noise down. We are fully booked today, there is no other room to transfer you to.

奧黛莉 我很抱歉,我現在馬上打電話上去請他們小聲一點。我們今天客滿,沒有空房可以換給你。

Sabrina I am very sorry. I had other complaints about the noise and we have asked the security to go and check on them. If you still want to transfer to a different room, I can check the availability for you.

莎賓娜 我很抱歉,其他的房客也有反應了,我有請保全上去看,如果你待會還想換房間的話,那我幫您看看空房狀況。

Dexter I am sorry to hear that. I will relay this to the guest and I will have a room ready for you to transfer in the next 30 minutes.

🔊

戴斯特 我很抱歉，我會向房客反應，請給我半個小時，我馬上幫您安排房間。

😋 字彙表

keep the noise down	小聲一點
fully booked	客滿
availability	空房情況
relay this to	向某人反應

MEMO

超實用短句 1

❶ 排水孔上有頭髮。

⇨ There are hairs on the drain.

❷ 房間的地板上還有非常多沙。

⇨ The floor of the room is very sandy.

❸ 馬桶沒有刷乾淨。

⇨ The toilet is not cleaned properly.

❹ 這房間有股臭味。

⇨ The room is very stinky.

🔔 超實用短句 2

❶ 垃圾沒有倒掉。

⇨ The trash was not emptied out.

❷ 桌子上都是灰塵。

⇨ The table is very dusty.

❸ 這地毯沒有吸。

⇨ The carpet needs to be vacuumed.

❹ 浴室的浴簾都發霉了。

⇨ The shower curtain is moldy.

MEMO

Q33 Do you have any feedback for us regarding your stay?

您對此次的住宿經驗有沒有意見？

Audrey　I think the bathroom and toilet needed to be aired out. It has a very strong moldy smell. It almost set off my allergies.

奧黛莉　我覺得浴室跟廁所需要通風，裡面有股很濃的霉味，我差一點過敏就發作了。

Sabrina　I want to make a complaint about the floor carpet; I think the carpet needs to be washed. There are lots of stains on the carpet.

莎賓娜　我覺得地板改進，地毯需要清洗，因為上面都是污漬。

Dexter Everything was alright other than the sheets. I think they need to be replaced; there were holes and stains on them. I was very disappointed.

戴斯特 除了床單之外我覺得其他都還好，床單實在非常需要換新的，都破洞了還有污漬。

字彙表

feedback	意見、回應
air out	通風
vacuum	吸塵
disappointed	很令人失望

飯店年久失修

🔔 超實用短句 1

❶ 洗手台的水龍頭在滴水。

⇨ The tap in the washing basin is dripping.

❷ 門鎖壞掉了，請派人來修理。

⇨ The door lock is broken, please get the maintenance to come and fix it.

❸ 窗戶沒辦法關緊，它卡住了。

⇨ The window doesn't shut properly. It is jammed.

❹ 冷氣吹出來的是熱風。

⇨ The air condition is blowing out hot air.

🔔 超實用短句 2

❶ 電燈一閃一閃的，需要換新的燈管。

⇨ The light is flickering. It needs to be replaced.

❷ 電視的音量很小，沒有辦法開大。

⇨ I can't turn up the TV volume. It is very quiet.

❸ 窗簾沒有辦法完全閉合。

⇨ The curtain does not shut properly.

❹ 這個床墊凹陷了，非常不舒服，應該要換新的。

⇨ The mattress is dented, and it was very uncomfortable.
Please replace with a new one.

MEMO

Q34 What is wrong with your room?

請問一下您的房間有什麼問題？

Audrey　I am having a problem with the ceiling light. The light is flickering. Can you send the maintenance guy up to replace it please?

奧黛莉　我的頂燈有問題，燈管一閃一閃的，麻煩你請維修工人來幫我換好嗎？

Sabrina　The mattress is terrible! I can't stand it, and it desperately needs to be replaced. Can you move me to a room with a better mattress please?

莎賓娜　這個床墊實在太糟了！我受不了，你們真的需要換一張新的。可以幫我換到有好一點的床墊的房間嗎？

Dexter The air conditioner is blowing out hot air and my room feels like a sauna. Can you please get someone to come and have a look?

戴斯特 這個冷氣吹出來的是熱風，我的房間向個蒸籠一樣。可以派人來看一下嗎？

字彙表

turn it up	開大聲
flickering	一閃一閃
mattress	床墊
blow out	吹出

MEMO

飯店鬧鬼

🔔 **超實用短句 1**

❶ 有人在我耳邊講話。
⇨ I can hear whispering in my ear.

❷ 我聽到浴室有聲音。
⇨ There was noise coming from the bathroom.

❸ 我覺得有人在床邊看著我。
⇨ There is someone staring at me by the bed.

❹ 我聽到腳步聲。
⇨ I heard footsteps.

🔔 超實用短句 2

❶ 有人敲門，可是開門後門口沒人。

⇨ Someone was knocking on the door, but there was no one there when I open the door.

❷ 我有看到一個人影。

⇨ I saw a shadow.

❸ 我發誓我沒有騙人。

⇨ I swear I was not lying.

❹ 我的房間有鬼。

⇨ My room is haunted!

MEMO

Q35 Why do you have to change to a different room?

為什麼你一定要換房間？

Audrey　The room just doesn't feel right. I could hear noise coming out of the bathroom. It sounded like someone is singing. I don't want to go back there.

奧黛莉　房間就不太對勁，我隱約聽到廁所有聲音，好像有人在唱歌，我不要回去那間房。

Sabrina　I swear there was a woman watching me sleep right by my bed. I could see a shadow then it disappeared. Can you go with me to pack my bags?

莎賓娜　我發誓有個女人在床邊看著我睡覺，我看到有個影子，然後他就不見了。你可以跟我回去打包行李嗎？

Dexter I turned everything off. Then I went to bed. All of sudden the TV turned itself back on. I got a fright then and just rushed out.

戴斯特 我把東西都關掉然後就去睡了，突然間電視自己打開，我嚇一跳就衝出來了。

字彙表

doesn't feel right	覺得不對勁、怪怪的
come out of	從哪裡出來
all of sudden	突然間
rushed out	衝出來

MEMO

國家圖書館出版品預行編目(CIP)資料

圖解一次學好餐飲英語會話+句型/ 陳幸美
著 -- 初版. -- 臺北市：倍斯特, 2018.12 面 ;
公分. -- （職場英語系列 ; 8）
ISBN 978-986-97075-0-3（平裝附光碟）
1.英語 2.餐飲業 3.會話 4.句法

805.188   107020165

職場英語 008

圖解一次學好餐飲英語會話+句型(附MP3)

初　　版　　2018年12月
定　　價　　新台幣380元

作　　者　　陳幸美
出　　版　　倍斯特出版事業有限公司
發 行 人　　周瑞德
電　　話　　886-2-2351-2007
傳　　真　　886-2-2351-0887
地　　址　　100 台北市中正區福州街1號10樓之2
E - m a i l　　best.books.service@gmail.com
官　　網　　www.bestbookstw.com
執行總監　　齊心瑀
責任編輯　　陳韋佑
封面構成　　盧穎作
內頁構成　　菩薩蠻數位文化有限公司
印　　製　　大亞彩色印刷製版股份有限公司

港澳地區總經銷　　泛華發行代理有限公司
地　　址　　香港新界將軍澳工業邨駿昌街7號2樓
電　　話　　852-2798-2323
傳　　真　　852-2796-5471